THE SKY PHANTOM

Nancy goes to the Excello Flying School in the Midwest to take lessons, while her friends Bess and George perfect their horseback riding. At once the young sleuth is confronted with the mystery of a hijacked plane and a missing pilot. Then the rancher's prize pony, Major, is stolen. Nancy becomes a detective in a plane and on horseback to track down the elusive sky phantom and the horse thief. A lucky find—a medal with a message to be deciphered on it—furnishes a worthwhile clue. Romance is added to mystery when Bess becomes interested in a handsome cowboy. Readers will spur Nancy on as she investigates a strange magnetic cloud, hunts for the horse thief, and finally arrives at a surprising solution.

"Untie me!" the cowboy demanded.

NANCY DREW MYSTERY STORIES®

The
Sky Phantom

BY CAROLYN KEENE

GROSSET & DUNLAP
Publishers • New York
A member of The Putnam & Grosset Group

PRINTED ON RECYCLED PAPER

Contents

The Sky Phantom

CHAPTER I

The ELT Signal

"PULL back on the stick, Nancy!" Bruce Fisher ordered.

Nancy Drew, an attractive strawberry blond, was taking a flying lesson from one of the new instructors at the Excello School, located in the Midwest. She and her friends Bess Marvin and George Fayne were spending their vacation at the nearby Hamilton Ranch. The other two girls were on the range, horseback riding.

"Very good, Nancy!" said Bruce. "But one thing you must remember. An airplane is a temperamental bird and must be treated gently. Take it easy and the plane will work with you."

Nancy had run into turbulent air and the plane had become difficult to control. Now she zoomed upward to gain altitude and avoid being tossed around. Presently she saw a very large cloud looming ahead.

"That's the mystery cloud," said her teacher. "You can get lost in there it's so big."

The word "mystery" caught Nancy's attention. To her the cloud looked like any other, but now it was the only one in the sky, which was blue and sunny. She asked why he called this particular vapory mass a mystery cloud.

Bruce explained, "Because it's there all the time—that is, this one or one just like it. This is a strange phenomenon."

"You mean the cloud never dissipates?" Nancy asked.

Bruce nodded. "I guess it's here continuously because of the high hills in this area. Meteorologists say that type of cloud formation is caused by orographic uplift."

Nancy chuckled. "That's a big word to remember."

As she flew closer to the cloud, Bruce said, "Now turn away from it. It could be dangerous."

Flying low, Nancy banked the plane. While in the turn, she looked below. To her surprise she saw her friends Bess, in a bright-red bandanna, and George, wearing green jodhpurs. They had reined in and were standing still, waving their arms wildly.

"I believe the girls are trying to signal me," Nancy told her instructor. "I wonder why. Maybe something's wrong!"

Bess Marvin, who was blond, pretty, and

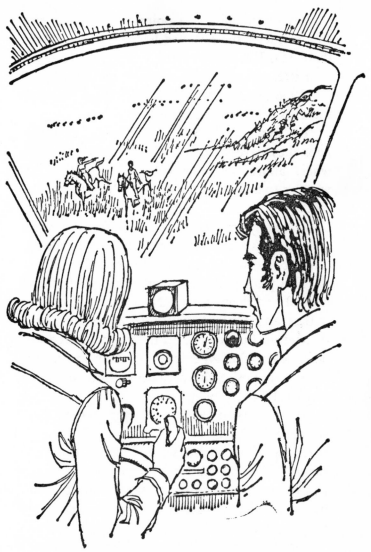

"The girls are trying to signal me!" Nancy said.
"Maybe something is wrong."

slightly overweight, was pointing up to the sky. In a moment, she swooped her arm down toward the earth. Her cousin George, a slender, athletic brunette, went through the same motions.

"What are they trying to say?" Bruce asked as the girls repeated the gesture.

"It's my guess," Nancy answered, "that perhaps they have spotted a plane in trouble somewhere above the other side of that hill. They want us to take a look. Let's see what we can find out."

Guided by her instructor, she banked and made several turns around the area, but neither she nor Bruce could see a plane on the ground.

"The pilot must have gotten his plane under control and flown away," Nancy remarked.

Bess and George continued to motion with their arms, but the two in the plane noticed that now, when the girls lowered their arms, they pointed opposite the area where Bruce's plane was circling.

"I'll see if I can pick up anything on the radio," Bruce said.

He switched on his set and began tuning to various frequencies. Nancy could catch bits of weather reports and airport instructions to incoming craft. Then Bruce suddenly stopped at one frequency.

"Do you hear that beeping?" he asked Nancy. She nodded.

Bruce said, "That usually means someone is in distress. Maybe your friends did see a plane out of control, and it went down in a place where we haven't looked."

Nancy remarked it might be a long hunt before they could find a craft on the ground. "Do we have enough fuel?" she asked.

Bruce smiled and said, "Yes. It may take us a little while, but by using this ELT signal, we can probably shorten the time."

He explained that ELT meant Emergency Locator Transmitter. "We'll fly in a search pattern and listen to those beeps. The stronger they are, the closer we're getting to the source. If they become weaker, then we're flying away and should turn back."

Nancy said to him, "You'd better take over. I'll look out the window."

Bruce flew directly south. The varying volume of the beeping sound reminded Nancy of a game she played as a child. She would search for a hidden object and her father would indicate that she was "hot," meaning close, or "cold," meaning not close.

After flying a few miles, Bruce banked sharply and took a northerly direction. The beeps were faint now, so he swung to the west. Here the signals were even fainter. He banked and went directly east.

Presently Nancy cried out, "There it is! I see

it. I wonder if the pilot is inside." She saw no one outside the craft and no signs of a parachute.

Just ahead, in a scrubby area near the base of a high hill was a small two-engine plane. The sleek-looking craft was painted a dull silver. Above it loomed the great cloud.

Bruce prepared to land near the craft. "This is the part I always hate to undertake," he said soberly. "There's no telling what we may find. Suppose I come down a distance away and you stay in the plane while I investigate?"

Nancy sighed. "You're my instructor, so I presume I'll have to obey your orders, but I'm asking you to let me go along. Please. I may be able to help."

Bruce shrugged and said, "Okay. But I insist on looking inside the plane first."

He brought the flying school's two-seater down to very rough, slightly sloping terrain. He did it so skillfully, though, that his passenger was not shaken. The two got out and walked toward the other plane.

"There's no sign of life," Bruce remarked with set lips.

Finally the couple reached the craft. The ELT signal was still beeping. Bruce climbed aboard. To their amazement, no one was in the plane or anywhere near it!

"Could the pilot have bailed out?" Nancy asked.

Bruce shook his head. "I doubt it. In that case, the plane would have crashed. As you can see, it didn't, and everything is in perfect order. No doubt it was a hard landing, however, and that may have triggered the ELT." Bruce paused, then said, "If the pilot heard it, I can't see why he didn't turn off his radio."

Nancy suggested that perhaps he was in such a hurry to go somewhere that he had not bothered. Bruce said this could be true. Possibly the pilot met and dashed away with a friend.

"He may even have had his ELT on while still flying and didn't bother to turn it off when he landed," Bruce added.

Nancy had already made a mental note of the plane's registration numbers on the fuselage. "Have you any idea whose plane it is?" she asked.

"No. But I'll climb inside and see if I can find any identification."

The nimble young instructor looked through every compartment in the craft. Finally he reported from the doorway, "Nothing about an owner or whoever was flying the plane. The pilot must be carrying the registration and airworthiness certificates with him. That's a violation of FAA rules, by the way."

Nancy thought, "He means Federal Aviation Agency."

Bruce looked down at Nancy. "I understand you like to solve mysteries. Here's one for you.

Who was the pilot of this plane, why did he land here, and where is he?"

The girl detective grinned. "If you'd like to know who the owner is, I'm sure I could find out."

They both laughed, and he said, "Go to it!"

The two walked back to the flying-school plane and Bruce immediately contacted the tower at Excello. He gave the registration numbers of the mysterious plane and asked if they could identify the owner or pilot. In a little while the answer came.

"The owner and pilot of the plane you asked about is Roger Paine. He purchased the craft only two weeks ago. It seems he left for the East in his old plane a few days before that, and no one has heard from him since. We're a bit concerned about him because he said he expected to return in a few days."

Nancy and Bruce looked at each other. Though Bruce had never met him, both of them knew Roger Paine was well liked at the Excello School and was considered "a great guy."

Nancy said, "The last time I visited this area I took a couple of lessons from Roger. He's a wonderful person. Oh, I hope nothing has happened to him!"

CHAPTER II

The Missing Palomino

By the time Nancy and Bruce had taxied up to the operations building of the Excello Flying School, the place was buzzing with excitement over Roger Paine's disappearance.

Mr. Falcon, the manager, had already telephoned the young man's home in the East. "I was told that no one in the family has heard from him for over two weeks. This isn't like him because he worked with his father part-time and was expected home. I also phoned several of the larger airports to see if I could track Roger down, but no luck."

According to various Excello pilots, Roger was not secretive. He visited the school once in a while and sometimes gave a few lessons.

"He's a top-notch airman," said one of the instructors. "If he wasn't injured in a crash, he must be in some other sort of trouble."

Nancy whispered to Bruce, "Couldn't a few of us start a search?"

He relayed her question to Mr. Falcon.

"I think that's a very good idea," the manager said. "It's too late to do it today. Sunset is less than an hour away. I suggest you start out at dawn tomorrow. Who wants to volunteer?"

Several pilots raised their hands, indicating they were willing to go.

Again Nancy whispered to Bruce, "May I join the search?"

He looked at her and smiled. Then he said, "Mr. Falcon, I'd like to introduce Nancy Drew, who is an amateur detective. But she's an amateur only because she won't accept money for her work. She is a marvelous sleuth, and she'd like to go with us."

The other men in the room clapped and Mr. Falcon said, "If Bruce wants to come, you may fly with him, Nancy. And good luck in your search."

"Oh, thank you," the girl replied. "What time is dawn tomorrow?"

Four A.M. was the answer. "Better set your alarm," Mr. Falcon added with a smile.

Nancy promised to do so and walked out with Bruce. He offered to drive her to the Hamilton Ranch, only a few miles from the airfield. On the way they continued to discuss what might have happened to Roger Paine.

Bruce said, "If he had a hard landing and bumped his head, he may have suffered a concussion and be wandering around aimlessly in those hills."

Nancy had a new and disturbing thought about the disappearance.

"I hate to say this," she said, "but it's just possible that Roger skipped out on purpose for reasons known only to himself. But the question is why? And where is he?"

Bruce said he did not believe that had happened. "It's possible, though, that Roger met with foul play in some way. Perhaps he had a passenger who was in some kind of tricky business and double-crossed him."

By this time the couple had reached the Hamilton Ranch and driven up to the long, logwood one-story house. They were greeted by Bess and George, who had met Bruce that morning.

"Did you find the plane we were pointing to?" George asked. "The pilot seemed to be in trouble."

"Yes, we did," Nancy replied and told them about Roger Paine and that his plane had been abandoned.

"How dreadful!" Bess remarked. "What kind of man was Roger Paine?"

"Young, handsome, and very friendly," Nancy said. "You'd like him."

"Most of the pilots at Excello know him,"

Bruce added, "and they're all fond of him." He turned his car and waved good-by.

Nancy followed Bess and George into the comfortably furnished lobby with its huge stone fireplace. Everywhere on the walls hung pictures of cowboys and Indians, and over the fireplace was a mural showing stampeding Brahman cattle.

The girls shared a large room, furnished with three cots. Nancy went to bed early and set her alarm for 3:30 A.M. When it buzzed, she instantly smothered the clock and turned it off so that Bess and George would not be awakened.

Nancy dressed quickly in her jeans and a sweater and left the room. Bruce was waiting for her at the front entrance.

"Morning!" he said. "Congratulations! I never thought you'd make it!"

Nancy chuckled. "You have a lot to learn about detectives. Hours mean nothing to us."

"I stand corrected," he said, as they drove off.

At the flying school she found that four planes were to take part in the search. Nancy and Bruce were to be in the lead, since they knew where Roger Paine's plane had set down. As they approached the area the great cloud seemed larger than ever.

"It's amazing," Nancy said.

"You know, you can get lost inside that cloud," Bruce remarked. "And sometimes our compass needles go crazy if we get too close."

"Then I'll be sure to stay away," Nancy replied, and she decided to make inquiries about it.

In a few minutes they thought they were over the spot where the missing aircraft had stood. It was not there! Bruce began to circle the area. "I was so sure I remembered exactly where it was," he said, a puzzled frown creasing his forehead.

"I thought so, too," Nancy agreed.

The pilot picked up his unicom transceiver and got in touch with the other fliers. He asked if they had seen the abandoned plane, but none of them had.

"We'll change our search pattern," Bruce directed. "I'll fly around the big cloud. Number two plane will go in a larger circle, and three and four beyond that, so we can cover a sizable area. If you see the craft, be sure to report to me at once."

The search went on for some time. Nancy kept her eyes glued to the ground, but there was no sign of a plane, a pilot, a house, or any type of building that might be used as a hideaway.

Nancy said, "Even if the plane is gone, maybe Roger isn't. Couldn't we go down and hunt for him on the ground? We might pick up a clue to the disappearance of the plane even if we don't find him."

Bruce agreed that this was a good idea and radioed the other pilots to return to the school.

"Nancy and I are going to conduct a ground search," he said. "We'll keep in touch."

The instructor made a perfect landing on the

uneven ground and stopped at the spot where he and Nancy were sure Roger Paine's plane had landed. They began to inspect the area and in a few minutes Nancy said, "Here are some wheel marks and imprints of cowboy boots!"

Bruce said he was sure they had not been there the day before. Nancy agreed. She added, "Roger didn't wear cowboy boots when he was giving me lessons."

"None of the pilots wear them," Bruce said thoughtfully.

"Then whose marks are these?" Nancy asked. "Maybe they belong to a skyjacker!" she surmised.

"It sure is a puzzle," Bruce replied.

The couple hunted for further clues but found none. There was no trail either from or to the cowboy-boot prints. How had their wearer reached the spot?

"He must have parachuted down," Nancy concluded, and Bruce agreed that this could be the answer to the riddle. "And immediately removed the boots."

The couple flew back to the Excello Flying School. This time Nancy took the controls. She made such a good landing that Bruce praised her skill.

"You're getting along great," he said.

Nancy thanked him and confessed that she was really terribly excited now about flying. "I just can't wait to get permission to make a cross-country flight."

Bruce said he felt this could happen soon. "In fact," he added, "I have a hunch that you're going to do some exciting flying in connection with this mystery before you solve it."

Nancy's blue eyes sparkled. "Great!" she said. "That would suit me."

When she reached the ranch, Nancy expected Bess and George to be there to ask about her progress. They were gone and there was no one else around the ranch house.

"I wonder where everyone is?" Nancy thought.

At this moment she heard loud voices coming from the large corral behind the barn. She turned and followed the sound. Nearly all the cowboys were there. The ranch owner, affectionately called Pop Hamilton, was talking to them.

Bess and George were leaning over the fence, listening to Pop. He asked with a kindly but authoritative ring to his voice, "Who was the last person to see Major?"

Nancy scooted over to where her friends were standing and asked what had happened.

Bess replied, "You know Major, Pop's beautiful palomino? Well, he's missing and he couldn't have run away because last night he was in a locked stall."

"You mean," said Nancy, "that somebody broke in and stole Major?"

George nodded. "That's what the men think. Pop is furious. He's a deputy sheriff and is going right after the thief."

Bess remarked that there were dogs on the place but no one had heard them barking. "So many mysterious things have happened," she added. "In two days, a strange cloud, an abandoned plane, and now a stolen palomino."

Thoughts were racing through Nancy's mind. Two ideas seemed to click. Cowboy shoe prints had been found where the mysterious plane had last been seen. Apparently there had been no disturbance on the ranch when the horse disappeared. Was it possible that Major knew the thief and this was why the pony had not caused a disturbance and why the dogs had not barked? Had the thief ridden the animal away from the ranch and sold it to someone else? If so, how had he reached the ranch? By parachute? And could he have taken both the pony and the aircraft?

Aloud, Nancy said to the other girls, "Roger Paine's abandoned plane was gone when we went to look at it again."

"What!" Bess and George exclaimed together.

Nancy explained, and then told them that she believed a parachutist might be working in the vicinity.

Bess wagged her head. "It sounds fantastic to me," she said. "But, Nancy, you're more often right than wrong, so I suppose it could be so."

She giggled. "Question: Did the cowboy take the palomino in the parachute with him and carry Major off in the plane?"

All three girls laughed, and returned to the house. When Pop Hamilton entered, he immediately went to his office to make some phone calls. He asked neighboring ranchers if anyone had seen Major.

The palomino was well known since he had been seen at parades during rodeos. Unfortunately, no one had seen Major lately, and he had not joined their own horses and cow ponies.

When the girls reached their room George said, "Since we have been here, Nancy, you have spent hardly any time with us. Couldn't you take one day off from your flying lessons and stay with us? We'd love to go on a long horseback ride. What do you say?"

Nancy put her arms around the two cousins. "I didn't realize it. You're absolutely right. I'll call Bruce at once and tell him I'll skip tomorrow's lesson and go out with you girls all day. We can take along a lunch."

The two cousins squeezed Nancy; then she went to the phone and got in touch with her instructor. She asked to be excused from her lesson the following day.

"On one condition," Bruce said. "You must spend an hour on your book work. The day after tomorrow I'll give you a quiz."

Nancy agreed and directly after lunch began to study. An hour later Bess and George walked into their room.

"How about giving me an examination?" Nancy asked. She grinned. "Or better yet, how about my asking you some questions?"

"I'm game," Bess replied, "but I'll flunk with a big zero."

"Here goes," Nancy said. "When you're flying over an airport and see a large white X at the end of one of the runways, what does it indicate?"

George grinned. "If it's the end of the runway, it's not the beginning. So I suppose you'd better stay off it."

"Good guess," Nancy told her. "It means that particular runway is out of use."

Bess declared that she was next and waited for Nancy's question.

"Here it is," Nancy said. "When flying in very turbulent air, or high winds, what is the first thing you should do?"

Bess giggled. "Reach for an airsick pill."

George scoffed. "You're supposed to take those before the trip, not during it!"

Neither she nor Bess could guess the answer, so Nancy told them. "Reduce your air speed by throttling back."

She promised that the next day she would ask them some more questions.

George said, "Oh no you don't! You'll give us

the book and we'll see if *you* know the answers!"

"Okay," Nancy agreed.

The following morning there was still no news of the missing palomino. The girls told Pop Hamilton they were planning to take a picnic lunch and ride out into the countryside to see if they could pick up any clues to the pony's disappearance. He was grateful for the suggestion and wished them luck.

When the girls started out after breakfast, Nancy wanted to go toward the site of the abandoned plane.

"We have no idea which way Major went or was taken, so let's go along the road first and then strike off toward the great-cloud area."

On the way the three girls rode slowly, their eyes searching the flat and hilly landscape for clues—hoofprints, footprints, or anything that might identify a thief. They had ridden about three miles from the Hamilton Ranch without noticing anything suspicious, when Nancy suddenly cried out, "Girls! Look!"

CHAPTER III

Revealing Rerun

BESS and George pulled up their mounts and gazed in the direction in which Nancy was pointing. Caught on some hillside bushes was a large piece of white cloth.

"That could be a parachute," Nancy stated. She urged her horse into a lope and headed for the spot. Bess and George followed close behind.

"It *is* a parachute!" George exclaimed. "Do you think somebody is under it?"

The three girls dismounted and tethered their ponies. They walked forward.

The parachute was spread unevenly across the ground and a couple of low bushes. Fearfully, Nancy and George lifted it. Bess had turned her back and closed her eyes. She waited for the others to tell her what they had found.

George winked at Nancy, then said, "Oh my goodness, there's a dinosaur under here!"

Bess turned around sheepishly. "Okay, okay!" she said. "Is *anything* under there?"

"Nothing," Nancy replied. Her attention returned to the parachute. "I'm sure that whoever landed in this chute wanted to do so without being spotted," she said.

"Then he managed to do just that," George remarked. "If anyone around here had seen a parachute coming down, we certainly would have heard about it."

"That's not what puzzles me," Nancy replied. "At night a chute is hard to spot. But after landing, why didn't the jumper gather up the canopy and bury or hide it in the brush? Why leave it spread out across the ground for anyone to see?"

"Maybe he was scared off," Bess suggested.

"Yes," Nancy agreed. "Possibly the sound of a horse or car approaching caused him to panic."

"Then," George added, "he ran off and forgot about hiding his chute."

Bess walked around. Some distance on the far side of the parachute she discovered two narrow tracks with heel marks. After studying them a moment, she concluded that the parachute had dragged the flyer backward a few feet. She called to the other girls to come and look. Bess explained what she thought the marks indicated.

"Good for you!" Nancy said. "I'm sure you're absolutely right."

Bess now ran ahead beyond the heel marks but

could see nothing more to explain what had happened. Meanwhile, Nancy and George searched the area around the chute but found no shoe marks. Bess returned to say she had discovered nothing.

"This is strange," Nancy said. "How did the chutist get away from here?"

She got down on her knees and examined the earth carefully. At last the young sleuth detected a slightly matted path and, a few feet beyond it, imprints of cowboy boots. She called the others.

Instantly George said, "The parachutist must have removed his boots and walked for a distance in his stocking feet before putting his boots back on. The imprints don't go far because the ground is hard."

Nancy nodded. "These footprints, by the way, look exactly the same as the ones I found at Roger Paine's plane. I'm going to measure these."

She hurried back to her pony and opened the saddlebag. She took out her camera, a tape measure, and a notebook. Then the young sleuth rejoined her friends.

Nancy focused the camera on the bootprints, taking several closeups from different angles. She handed the camera to Bess and requested her to take some snapshots of the parachute.

"Okay," Bess said. "I'll try it from the top, from far away, and close by."

While she was gone, George made various measurements of the cowboy bootprints with the tape measure. Nancy wrote them in her notebook, then drew a little sketch.

George remarked, "It's lucky we found these prints before rain washed them away."

"Yes," said Nancy, "and I hope it won't rain before we have a chance to compare them with the bootmarks we found near Roger Paine's plane."

Bess returned and handed the camera to Nancy. "I used up the roll," she said. "Do you have another one with you?"

Nancy nodded, then urged that they ride on toward the area under the big cloud.

"Please, not yet!" Bess pleaded. "I'm starving! There's a nice tree with shade on the hillside. Why don't we eat our picnic lunch now?"

Nancy glanced at her watch. She was amazed to find that so much time had gone by. It was long after midday.

"I guess you're right," she said.

The ponies were moved to a shady spot and given water from their own saddlebags.

"I hope there are chicken sandwiches in our lunch," said Bess as the girls carried up the boxes packed in the Hamilton kitchen.

Her wish was granted and Bess grinned as she started to eat. She was the first one to finish and lie down on the grass. In a moment her eyes closed and she fell asleep.

Nancy and George discussed their next move. The young sleuth still wanted to ride on to the spot where she and Bruce had discovered Roger Paine's plane and compare the mysterious footprints.

George thought it was too late. "We're a long way from there and couldn't get back to the ranch until after dark," she objected.

Another thought came to Nancy. "Perhaps we should ride to Excello and report what we found here," she said. "Maybe someone at the school will know about the chutist."

George leaned over and shook Bess. "Wake up, sleepyhead," she said. "Detectives don't take naps while working!"

"Who's working?" Bess countered. "I thought we were eating lunch."

Nevertheless, she stood up when the other girls did and walked with them to their ponies. Bess was told of the decision to go to Excello and inquire about a parachutist.

Nancy added, "After that we'd better hurry to the ranch and tell Pop Hamilton. Remember, the chutist could have been the one who walked to the ranch and left with Major without being noticed."

Bess added, "Don't forget that there's a dance

at the ranch house tonight. I wouldn't want to miss it for anything."

"That's right," George agreed. "And I suppose Chuck Chase will be there, chasing you again."

Bess blushed. She was afraid that George might object to her interest in the cowboy because of Bess's friend Dave, back home. He was never pleased when she dated other boys.

When the girls reached Excello, Nancy asked Mr. Falcon and the pilots who were around if anyone knew of a parachutist who had landed in the vicinity recently. None of them did.

The State Police were contacted. Up to now, they had not heard anything about a person landing in their territory. Nancy was disappointed.

Just then Bruce walked in. "Did you have a pleasant day?" he asked.

Nancy told him what the young detectives had discovered and he was amazed, but like the other pilots had no explanation.

"By the way," he said, "would you three like to watch a movie of student performances?"

"Oh, we'd love to!" Nancy replied.

In a few minutes the girls and the pilots were looking at some of the footage. Presently there was one of Nancy about to climb into the cockpit. First she brushed off her clothes, then smoothed down her hair.

Bess whispered to her, "Don't you ever tease

me again about trying to look pretty before going on a date!"

Nancy chuckled as she watched herself board the plane and take the pilot's seat. She started the engine and taxied down the runway.

Then the man operating the projector apparently decided to have some fun. Nancy, in a lightning move, turned the plane around and taxied back at terrific speed. Reaching the starting point, she switched once more and zipped down the runway. The pilots in the room roared with laughter.

"Fastest takeoff on record!" one of them teased.

"My goodness," said Bess, "how fast were you going?"

Nancy explained that the man showing the picture was playing a joke. "Actually I was proceeding very slowly," she said.

At this moment her attention was directed to another student, who was flying at a good clip alongside the great cloud. A larger plane was coming toward him and for a few moments it looked as if there would be a crash. Then, without warning, the oncoming pilot rolled into a diving turn to get below the student and vanished into the cloud.

Nancy was sitting on the edge of her chair. "Maybe that's the mystery pilot!" she said to her friends. "Perhaps he hides in the clouds so he won't be recognized!"

The movie continued for several minutes, but

the plane that had disappeared did not appear again. The film focused on another student.

When the movie was over, Nancy requested a rerun of the scene with the mystery pilot. The operator replayed that part of the film.

The young detective tried hard to make out the letters and numbers of the oncoming plane, but could not distinguish them. She felt sure, however, that the sleek craft was the same one she and Bruce had found in the wilderness. Unfortunately, the film was black and white, so she could not tell what color the craft was.

"Thank you," she called out to the operator.

When the meeting was over, Nancy went to the desk and inquired if there had been any news of Roger Paine.

"Not yet," was the answer. "We called the police a short while ago to see if they had had any word, but no one seems to have heard from Roger."

Bruce walked the three girls to their ponies and said, "I'll see you tomorrow, Nancy."

She nodded. Then the riders galloped and returned to the Hamilton Ranch. They went at once to find Pop, who seemed very somber. There had been no word about his beloved Major.

After Nancy gave her report to Pop, he said he would send two boys out the following morning to search for the parachutist.

Late that afternoon an impromptu rodeo was

to be staged on the far side of one of the barns. There were chairs for the spectators, but no one used them. The events were too exciting for anyone to sit still!

At one end of the large corral a gate was set up through which contestants hurtled into the ring. The timer, a gray-haired cowboy, stood close to the gate, clutching his stop watch with serious concentration. Suddenly a familiar figure galloped into the corral with a lasso swinging.

"There's Chuck Chase!" Bess exclaimed. She fumbled nervously. "Oh, I hope he doesn't get hurt!"

Chuck had entered the calf-roping contest. Three cowboys ahead of him had brought their calves to the ground and tied them within seconds of one another. The last contestant had taken only thirty seconds, which was shorter than the other two. Now it was Chuck's turn.

As the calf was let onto the field, a man standing near the girls said to them, "That little critter is pretty ornery!"

This remark made Bess more nervous than ever. "Oh, don't get hurt, please!" she whispered.

Chuck's lariat snaked out and brought down the calf, which struggled to get up. The cowboy's nimble fingers worked like lightning. He had the calf's feet tied together in twenty-five seconds. He was the winner!

Everyone clapped and shouted. "Good work!"

Looking pleased, Chuck walked toward the au-
dience. He seemed to be searching for someone.
Finally he found Bess. Taking off his sombrero,
he tossed it directly at the girl, matador style. Bess
was so flustered she blushed a deep red. She knew
the gesture meant, "I choose you as my lady."

Nancy and George clapped and laughed, but
tears of happiness rolled down Bess's cheeks. She
finally managed to call out, "Oh, thank you,
Chuck. Thank you!"

As soon as the rodeo was over, everyone went
to supper. Later they gathered in the big mess hall
for a dance. The orchestra consisted of two guitars
and a banjo.

When the music started, Pop Hamilton led
Nancy onto the floor. For a couple of minutes,
there was no conversation.

Then the rancher said, "I'm trying to be sociable and have a good time. But between you and
me, I feel pretty sad about Major. Nancy, you're
a good detective. Please find him for me!"

Nancy smiled at the man. "I'm trying very hard
to do so," she said. "But there seem to be no clues
to the horse thief."

Again there was silence for a few minutes.
Then, as the music was about to stop, Pop said,
"This afternoon I received a strange phone call,
Nancy. For hours I have been debating with my-
self about whether or not I should tell you what
the message was."

"Is it bad news?" Nancy asked quickly.

"If you mean trouble at home, the answer is no," Pop replied.

"Then what is it?"

"Oh, well, I might as well tell you. I think it might directly concern you. This mystery man who called said, 'Keep that snoopy girl off my trail, or——' Nancy, could he have meant you?"

"Possibly. What else did he say?"

Pop Hamilton did not reply at once. He seemed to be debating with himself whether or not to give Nancy the rest of the message.

CHAPTER IV

Spooked!

WHEN the dance concluded, Nancy and Pop walked outdoors together. She said to him, "Please tell me the rest of the phone message that worried you."

"All right," he said. "The man who called threatened not only you but everyone else who dared to interfere with his plans."

"What are his plans?" Nancy asked.

She was not disturbed because she had been threatened many times before. The young sleuth figured that such people are usually cowards and invariably defeat their own purposes.

Pop Hamilton said the man had not told him anything else. "In fact, he hung up as soon as he had delivered his message."

"Was his voice familiar to you?" Nancy inquired.

Pop shook his head. "It was rather deep. He

spoke crisply and unpleasantly. I don't know any-one like that."

He patted Nancy on the shoulder. "I hope you won't worry about this. But promise me you will always have someone with you in case this stranger comes to bother you."

Nancy agreed, and the two walked back into the mess hall. In a moment, Nancy was claimed by another cowboy dancer, and spent the rest of the evening having a very good time with lots of jokes and laughter.

Later, she, Bess, and George prepared for bed. Nancy told the cousins what Pop had said and warned them to be very careful and never to travel alone anywhere.

George's eyes had a faraway look. "There's something really big going on in connection with this mystery," she said.

Bess was alarmed. "Oh, Nancy, why can't you ever solve a mystery without all sorts of threats and harrowing dangers to you, George, and me?"

Nancy did not reply. She merely smiled and brushed her hair vigorously. The next morning she was up early and off on horseback to the Ex-cello Flying School. It was not until she reached a lonely stretch of road that Nancy remembered her promise to Pop never to travel alone.

Now, however, there was no one in sight. She felt perfectly safe.

Suddenly, another horseman appeared around a curve. Nancy would meet him head-on! Would he be friendly or try to harm her?

The young sleuth's pulse began to throb. Should she race back to the ranch or take a chance? Nancy remembered that while flying she had seen an old road to the school. It led up over a hill. Quickly she pulled on her right rein and galloped across a field, then up the slope and among some trees. Now she was not visible to the other rider!

"What a relief!" she thought.

Nancy rode down the far side of the slope within sight of the airfield. She urged her pony on and within a short time reached the school.

Bruce was not there yet. The manager saw her and called Nancy to the desk. "Bruce telephoned," he explained, "and told me he would be late. He said if you wanted to use another instructor today, it would be okay."

"Thank you," Nancy said, and went over to sit down on a bench. She would wait for Bruce.

At this moment another pilot came up to her. He talked so fast, running all his words together, that she had no idea what he was saying.

"Sorry, but I didn't understand you," she interrupted.

Once more he spouted off at a dizzy speed. "I'm HalCalkin. Isaidmorninhiya. Swelldayforflying.

Howy'allfixedfortime. Lemmeseeyourlogbook."

Although it was hopeless to follow everything, she figured out that Hal Calkin was his name.

"Thanks very much, Hal," she said. "I'm waiting for Bruce."

Nancy concluded that even though Hal might be a good pilot, he would be an impossible instructor to understand. She had better not try it at this point in her lessons!

The affable Hal grinned and said, " 'tsokay. Wellgoodluck."

After he moved off, Nancy tried to recall what Hal had said. She had just about unscrambled his remarks, "Swell day for flying. How are you fixed for time? Let me see your logbook," when Bruce walked in. He hurried over to her.

"I'm so glad you waited. Well, I'm ready if you are."

"All set," she replied as they walked out to the airfield.

The morning's lesson was to practice steep turns and accelerated stalls. When they reached a wide-open area, Nancy took the plane up to 3,500 feet. Now she did a series of steep spirals.

"Very well done," said Bruce. "I think I'll try you on some ess-turns."

He pointed to a straight narrow river some distance ahead. "Use that as your pattern. Where is the wind now?"

"From the east," she replied.

Bruce instructed her to cross the stream. "When you reach the other side, your steepest bank will be required to take you on the first right turn of your ess. As you come back across the water, this will be the shallowest part of your second bank. You'll make a wide curve, then cross the stream again."

"And make another steep bank?" Nancy asked.

Bruce nodded, and with a grin said, "How many times do you think you could do this without becoming dizzy?"

Nancy chuckled. "What's the record?"

Bruce remarked that he would not dare tell her because she would try to beat it.

Smiling, he changed the subject. "We'll practice some eights-around."

Bruce explained to his student that the maneuver was performed at a fairly low altitude. She was to select two prominent points on the ground below spaced about two or three miles apart.

"In addition to this," her instructor added, "the axis between your selected ground points must be at a right angle to the wind."

"The wind is from the north," Nancy observed. "That means my ground points should be east and west."

"Good!" Bruce said. "Now the purpose of this maneuver is to teach you how to maintain a fixed radius, or distance, from your selected ground points while turning around them."

"I read about eights-around in my textbook," Nancy said. "If we could see our shadow moving across the ground, we'd see our plane making figure-eights between the two ground points."

Bruce was pleased. "You catch on fast," he told his student. "And remember! Shallow out the bank of your turn when flying upwind around the ground point, and steepen the bank when turning downwind."

Nancy completed the maneuver with a good score. She continued the turns until Bruce decided to call it a day. On the way back to Excello, Nancy flew directly over the site where Roger Paine's plane had landed, then mysteriously left again. Apparently, the craft had been taken away forever. But where was Roger Paine?

Nancy went on. Reaching the flying school's airstrip, the girl pilot came in for a smooth three-point landing.

"I've certainly enjoyed my lesson today," she said. "Thanks a lot. I came over on a pony, so I won't need a ride back."

Fortunately there were cars and other horsemen on the road as Nancy returned to the ranch, so she was not worried about anyone stopping her.

When she arrived, the young flier went to the girls' bedroom. Both of her friends were there.

Bess said, "Oh Nancy, you'll have to join us day after tomorrow! We have marvelous plans for you."

"What's up?" Nancy asked.

Bess told her that she had arranged with Pop Hamilton for an all-night pack trip on horseback. "Pop will go with us along with Chuck and Range Cooper." She giggled. "Range's real name is Wilfred, but he doesn't like it. Someone nicknamed him Range. He loves to be out on the range, rounding up strays."

George took up the story. "First we'll go to the place where you found the parachute, and make another search for Major and a chutist. Pop thinks the State Police might have overlooked some clue. He's determined to find his prize pony. Then we'll go on to the landing site of Roger Paine's plane."

Nancy said the trip sounded wonderful to her. "I can take a double lesson tomorrow to make up for the time we'll be away."

She phoned Bruce to ask if this were possible and he was happy to change her schedule.

The next morning, when Nancy and Bruce were airborne, she asked if they might go beyond the mystery spot during her lesson.

"Let's see if we can possibly find out anything to help explain the disappearance of Roger Paine," she pleaded. Nancy said she was more convinced than ever that there had been some kind of foul play, with a very good chance the vanished pilot had been hidden in this region.

"Maybe Roger Paine is being held captive inside the great cloud," Bruce commented with a smile.

The young detective, who had been considering every angle of the case, surprised him by saying, "I thought of that too and called a climatologist at the state university."

Bruce's eyes opened wide. "You told him you thought a man was trapped in a cloud?" he asked in amazement. "You don't really believe that's possible, do you?"

Nancy smiled when her instructor chuckled. "I wanted to know what, if any, investigation of the cloud had been done," she explained.

Bruce became serious again. "A great deal, I imagine."

"You're absolutely correct. The climatology department has thoroughly examined the cloud on two occasions. Apparently it is nothing more than a vapory mass protected by surrounding mountains, just as you told me."

Bruce admired Nancy's clear thinking and concluded she would make an excellent pilot. As she flew the plane, he requested her to go through various maneuvers. Only once did she make a bad mistake.

Feeling a bit overconfident, Nancy decided to show Bruce her mastery of steep turns. Rolling into a tight spiral she applied top rudder to prevent the nose of the plane from dropping too rapidly. This served only to aggravate the turn. In an effort to check her descent, Nancy pulled back violently on the stick. Suddenly, the plane snapped over in the opposite direction of the turn and entered a vicious spin.

"Wha-What's happening?" Nancy cried out.

"An over-the-top spin!" Bruce shouted. "The spin is to the right! Left rudder! Left rudder!"

Nancy quickly responded to his instructions. The moment the plane stopped spinning, she eased the stick forward and then carefully pulled it back, gradually recovering from the steep dive.

"It looks as if I've turned out to be a bad student," Nancy sighed.

"Nonsense!" Bruce declared. "You followed my instructions without a hitch. But you forgot a very important bit of advice. Go easy! Respect an aircraft—and the aircraft will respect you."

Some twenty minutes later the two fliers noted a lone horseman on a narrow trail they had not seen before. Nancy grabbed the binoculars and trained them on the man. He had his back to them and wore a large sombrero that hid his figure from view. But his pony was unmistakably a palomino!

"Maybe that's Major!" Nancy told Bruce. "Okay with you if we go down and find out?"

Bruce scanned the terrain. "That area is much too wild to land in. We'd ruin our craft."

"All right," said Nancy. "We won't try to land

—just trail that rider and get a better look at the horse. If it's Major, we can report the rider's location to the police."

She flew low. Unfortunately, it spooked the pony. He bolted off into the wild bush, with the man trying his best to bring the palomino under control. It was useless. Running senselessly, the horse was swift as the wind.

"Let's follow him!" Nancy cried out, excited.

CHAPTER V

Mistaken Identity

"OKAY," Bruce said. "Chase that pony, but stay high enough off the ground so we don't run into anything. And keep circling back so you won't lose him."

"Maybe you'd better take over," Nancy suggested, worried.

"No," was the reply, "you can do it. Just remember what you've learned."

Nancy kept her eyes on the racing palomino and its rider, watching the terrain ahead at the same time. The trail was a winding one. Once the animal disappeared into a forest area. Nancy circled the spot, hoping the rider would come out. He did not, but in an area of sparse trees she saw him. He was still galloping.

Bruce remarked, "That's some pony! He must have lungs like a giant bellows."

A few minutes later Nancy and Bruce saw the

horse and its rider appear from among the trees. The animal, now showing signs of exhaustion, was well under control. Finally he slowed down to a walk and then stopped.

To Nancy's delight, the spot was in a large grassy section. She could land safely!

With some coaching from Bruce, the girl flier brought the plane in on an excellent approach. She taxied near the animal as quietly as possible, watching carefully to see if he were going to spook again.

The rider was reassuring his mount, stroking the pony's neck and speaking to him in soothing tones. Although the animal was still trembling a bit he stood still, watching intently as the plane approached. Nancy and Bruce climbed out of the craft and walked forward.

"Hi," said Bruce. He looked to Nancy to give him some signal as to what to say next to this stranger.

The girl smiled at the rider. "I'm sorry I spooked your pony. I thought he was one that was stolen from the Hamilton Ranch, but I was wrong."

This animal did not have the same markings as Pop Hamilton's prize mount.

"You mean Major?" the man asked.

"Then you know about the theft?" Nancy asked.

The rider nodded and introduced himself as

Howard Stanton, a government agent. He showed his credentials, then said he was trying to track down Major and several other horses and ponies that had been stolen.

"But I'm afraid all of them are far away from here now," he said. "Horse thieves get their stolen animals out of the state and sell them as fast as they can."

After Nancy and Bruce were in the air again, she asked, "Did you agree with Mr. Stanton that thieves take stolen animals out of the state as quickly as possible?"

Bruce said he did. "It would seem foolish to keep them around here because they could be located easily."

Nancy did not entirely agree. "I don't know about all the stolen horses, but I have a strong hunch that Major is hidden somewhere close to the Hamilton Ranch."

Bruce smiled. "Which means that you would like to continue the search, combining it with your flying lesson."

"Exactly," Nancy told him.

As the young detective practiced, she and Bruce scanned the ground and used the binoculars every once in a while. There was no sign of Major or any other pony.

"Too bad," Nancy said. She was very disappointed at their failure to pick up any clues.

Finally pupil and instructor headed home. An

hour later, when Nancy reached the Hamilton Ranch, she found that Bess and George had been busy preparing for their pack trip on horseback the following day.

George said, "Bess and I will use the ponies we've been riding, Nancy. But you'll have to choose one. You'd better do it now so there won't be any delay in the morning."

As the girls approached the corral, Bess whispered, "That rough cowboy, Ben Rall, is in charge. I can't stand him."

Rall did not speak to the girls, just glared at them.

Nancy said, "I'd like to try out a pony to use in the ride tomorrow. Which one is gentle?"

"None of 'em when they get mad," Ben replied. He made no suggestion.

First Nancy chose a lovely sensitive-looking gray mare who responded immediately to her voice. Just as they were becoming friends, a beautiful two-month-old gray colt trotted around the corner of the corral and started nursing.

"Oh!" Nancy exclaimed. "So this lovely baby belongs to you? What a magnificent pair you are!"

"You think you're so smart," Ben snarled. "You're no cowgirl! You can't take a nursing mother away from her colt!"

Nancy blushed and stammered that she had just realized the gray had a colt. She picked another mare, which had kind eyes.

"That's Daisy D," George told her. "She's nice. You'll love riding her."

"All right," Nancy said. "I'll try her. Where do I find a saddle and blanket?"

The cowboy frowned at her, then said grudgingly, "Oh, I'll do it."

He led Daisy D into the stable. A few minutes later he brought out the pony. Nancy nodded her approval and vaulted into the saddle. She rode around the corral twice and was just about to say, "She'll be fine," when Daisy D reared up on her hind legs, nearly throwing her rider off.

Nancy tried her best to calm the pony, who came down on the ground with a thud, then began to run wildly. A few seconds later Daisy D jumped over the fence and bolted.

Nancy talked soothingly to the pony, while seesawing on the reins until she was afraid she would cut the animal's mouth. Finally, with a loud snort, Daisy D stopped. Nancy quickly dismounted and held the pony still.

Patting the animal's neck, she said, "You're all right, old girl. You're not hurt."

Nancy herself was not so sure of the latter statement. Bess and George rushed up and she said to them, "Take off the saddle and blanket. I suspect there's something underneath the blanket."

The girls did so, and Bess cried out, "There's a big bur under the blanket!"

George added, "No wonder she sunfished.

Those prickles went right into her flesh! The poor pony!"

Bess was furious. "I'm sure Ben Rall put that bur under the blanket on purpose. How mean can a person get?"

"I'm going to find out if he's responsible!" Nancy declared.

She stalked back toward the corral. Ben was not in sight. She hurried into the barn, but the cowboy was not there, either.

By this time George had led Daisy D up to the barn so that some soothing antiseptic salve could be put over the punctured flesh on her back.

Bess was even more upset about the incident than the other girls. When she found out Ben was not around, she went to look for Pete, the man in charge of the corral.

After Bess told Pete what had happened, he exclaimed, "There's no excuse for this! Every person who saddles a horse is supposed to inspect blankets and saddles carefully so nothing harmful will be put on a pony's back."

Bess looked at him. "We don't know why, but we think that Ben Rall put the bur there on purpose."

Pete yelled loudly for Ben, and finally the cowboy came. Pete showed him the bur and the puncture on the pony's back.

"How do you explain this?" he asked sternly.

Ben looked at the ground, then said, "I don't have to explain nothin'."

Daisy D suddenly sunfished.

"You explain," said Pete, "or you're all through at Hamilton Ranch!"

Instead of replying, Ben Rall turned and looked at Nancy. Glaring at her with anger in his eyes, he cried out, "I hate the city brand of a cowgirl who tries to fly planes and goes around nosing into everybody's business to solve mysteries. I'll get even with you for making me lose my job!" He waved a fist at her.

CHAPTER VI

A Puzzling Medal

NANCY stared after the retreating cowboy, realizing that she had unwittingly made an enemy. But what was the reason? She had never seen or heard of Ben Rall.

"He mentioned my being a detective. That's strange. Could he have had something to do with the mystery of the stolen palomino, or even with the disappearance of Roger Paine?" she asked herself.

To Pete she said, "What kind of a man is Ben Rall?"

"Very hard to get along with," was the answer. "He seems honest enough, but pretty ornery at times. The other boys don't care for Ben so they try to avoid him. I think this angers him, and then he's meaner than ever to everyone on the ranch.

"Some other tricks have been played around here, but we never could find out who did them.

After this bur incident, I'm beginning to wonder if Ben wasn't responsible for the other things, too. Well, I'm not sorry to see him go."

Bess asked in concern, "What will Ben do? Where will he go?"

Pete said that Pop Hamilton was generous to people he had to discharge.

"Usually they get a month's wages in advance and a good pony. I don't think it'll be hard for Ben to find a job on another ranch before he spends all his money."

This made the girls feel better, but Bess admitted she was afraid that Ben might try to harm Nancy.

"Oh, let's forget the whole incident," George Fayne said. "It disgusts me to think about it."

Nancy had little to say, but she decided to keep her eyes open for any trouble from the dismissed cowboy. She also decided that the next day she would inspect and saddle Daisy D without any assistance. She wanted no more sudden sunfishing by her pony!

Before breakfast the following morning, she went out alone to the barn, where Daisy D had been put into a stall. The pony wagged her head as the girl entered.

"How are you, pretty girl?" Nancy asked, stroking Daisy D's neck.

Apparently the pony liked this and nuzzled

the girl. Nancy examined the bur puncture on the animal's back. It was healing nicely.

Just then Pete came into the barn. "Morning, miss," he said. "You're out early!"

Nancy smiled and said she had a reason for getting up before the regular rising time at the ranch house.

"I thought I'd take Daisy D and see if riding bothers her."

Pete grinned. "Sort of a trial run, eh? Well, I don't blame you."

Nancy nodded and said she wondered if a protective bandage should be put over the pony's sore before a blanket and saddle were set in place. The cowboy agreed.

As he went to get a large antiseptic gauze, he called out, "You'll be glad to hear that Ben collected his wages and left last night. He went off on a pony Pop gave him."

"That was very generous," Nancy commented. She asked what the pony looked like and was told she was a sorrel with a broad band of white down her nose. The animal's front feet had large patches of white on them.

"She's pretty easy to identify," Pete remarked. "While you're riding, you'd better keep your eyes open for Ben and his pony."

"I certainly will," Nancy said.

She took a saddle pad from the shelf and examined it carefully. Finding it clean, smooth, and soft, she swung it across Daisy D's back, holding the gauze tightly in place. Then she located the comfortable saddle she had used the day before and put it on.

"Climb up," Pete said, "and I'll adjust the stirrups to exactly the right height. I noticed, Nancy, that you ride more in the English style than in our western type."

"Yes, I do," she replied.

Nancy got astride. The stirrups were adjusted properly. Then she gathered up the reins and squeezed the pony with her legs. They rode off at a brisk pace.

Daisy D proved to be a wonderful companion. She was affectionate and responded to the rider's slightest signal. Nancy walked, trotted, cantered, and galloped. Daisy D did not object. The girl detective returned to the barn, smiling.

"Daisy D is great," she said to Pete. "I can't wait to start on the pack trip."

He told her that the breakfast gong had already rung. "You'd better scoot to the mess hall," he advised with a grin. "I'll take care of Daisy D and give her some breakfast too."

"Thank you," Nancy answered, and she ran off toward the ranch house.

One hour later her group was ready to leave. An extra pony was being taken along to carry supplies. It was a gorgeous morning, and the six riders were exhilarated.

Chuck Chase rode with Bess and they seemed to be having a delightful time, laughing frequently. Range Cooper kept pace with George, while Nancy and Pop Hamilton led the group.

They followed the road for several miles, planning to turn off near the place where Roger Paine's plane had come down. Just before noontime Nancy spotted a lone rider in the distance. She pointed him out to Pop and the others.

The rancher looked ahead intently. "I wonder if that could be Ben Rall," he said. "If so, we'd better catch him! I found out this morning that he stole over a hundred dollars from the other men when he left!"

The rider disappeared around the bend. As the group reached the turn, they found a steep hillside on their left. Hoofprints indicated that the man on horseback had gone up to the top. The slope had little growing on it, but a dense growth of trees covered the peak.

Pop commanded, "Come on, boys! We'll see who that is! Girls, you stay here."

The three girls dismounted and held their ponies. Nancy and George looked out over the wide stretch of land in front of the hill. Bess stood still, gazing up to the top.

Suddenly she cried out, "Run, girls, run!"

Nancy and George spun around to see why. Looking up the slope, they saw a huge tree trunk tumbling down the steep incline directly toward them!

"Grab the ponies!" Nancy yelled.

Although Bess had given the signal, she now seemed paralyzed with fright and did not move. George grabbed their two ponies and dashed out of the way of the oncoming tree. Nancy reached for Bess's hand while clutching Daisy D's bridle, pulling her and Bess to safety.

The tree, coming at lightning speed, just missed them. It rolled for some distance along the flat area.

No one had been hurt!

Bess stood like someone transfixed, staring into space. Her cousin shook her. "What's the matter with you, Bess?" she asked. "Come to! The danger is over!"

Bess said she was sorry for not reacting faster after warning the others. "The reason was that I saw a face at the top of the hill leering down at us. I'm sure he started that tree rolling. And what's more, I think the man was Ben Rall, who threatened to hurt you, Nancy."

"If you're right," the girl sleuth replied, "I hope Pop and the boys capture him."

In a little while the other riders returned. The girls were sorry to see that the cowboy was not with them. Pop reported that they had not seen the lone rider.

"But I did!" Bess spoke up. "He tried to kill Nancy, George, and me!"

"What!" Pop, Chuck, and Range exclaimed together.

"That's right," George added. She told them what had happened. "You can see the evidence some distance from here." She pointed toward the tree that had rolled down the slope and onto the open area.

Pop commented, "That's a fine twist. Here I tell you to stay in this spot so you'll be safe, and you were the ones who were nearly killed while the boys and I didn't even get a glimpse of the culprit!"

Bess nodded. "If that was Ben Rall, he has already started to carry out his threat to get even with Nancy!"

The three men frowned. Pop said, "From now on we must take double precautions."

The group had lunch and rested a while, then set off again. It was almost dark when they reached the spot where Roger Paine's plane had landed. It was not there now. Had it been there and gone again? They all examined the ground but could not answer the question.

Later in the evening, they brought out their sleeping bags. When they were ready to climb into them, Chuck said, "I think we should set up guard. I'll take the first watch."

Pop Hamilton agreed and asked Chuck to awaken him three hours later.

Range Cooper grinned. "That makes me last, and my watch will run into breakfast time. I promise you all a great feast!"

The three girls offered to take turns watching, also, but the others wouldn't hear of it. They slept soundly and awoke to the aroma of sizzling bacon and hot biscuits.

"How heavenly!" Bess exclaimed, raising her arms to stretch. "Nothing ever smelled so good!"

The morning meal was as tasty as it smelled. Range, complimented by the girls, seemed embarrassed, and a red flush came over his sun-tanned face.

"It was nothing," he declared.

As soon as they had finished and tidied their little camp, Nancy was eager to start her search for a clue that would identify the sky phantom. She walked in ever-widening circles in order not to miss an inch of ground. An hour later, to her delight, she found something exciting. Nancy called to the other searchers to come and see what she had picked up.

"What did you find?" Pop asked.

"It's a silver medal with a chain attached to it," she said. "And look, the initials on it are R.P.!"

The others in the group were amazed. George

asked, "You believe the R.P. stands for Roger Paine?"

"I don't know," Nancy replied. "On the back of the medal is a series of strange marks."

Her friends rushed over to look at them.

Bess asked, "Do you suppose these marks are a clue that Roger left behind on purpose? Do you think that if we can figure out what they mean, we can find him?"

CHAPTER VII

Happy Discovery

THE RIDERS gathered around Nancy. She held up the silver medal, showing first the side containing the large engraved initials.

"Those must be Roger Paine's," George said. "It would be too much of a coincidence if they belonged to someone else."

Chuck asked to see what was on the back of the medal. Nancy turned it over.

The cowboy laughed. "Looks like Greek to me," he said.

Each one glanced at the strange markings, but no one could make any sense out of them.

Range asked, "If Roger Paine was abducted and left this as a clue, why didn't he put something on it that we can read?"

All this time Nancy had been staring intently at the back of the silver medal and the carefully made grooves on it.

Finally she said, "These markings are machine-cut, and he wouldn't have had any engraving apparatus out here!"

"You're absolutely right," Pop agreed.

Once again each member of the group took a turn studying the oddly formed characters, but still no one could venture a guess as to what they meant.

"Let's get on with our search!" George suggested impatiently.

Nancy put the medal in her pocket and once more the searchers separated, each one scanning the ground carefully for further bits of evidence.

"There must be something around here," Range murmured.

The search lasted nearly an hour before anyone made a discovery. Chuck and Bess had found some indistinct hoofprints that did not belong to any of the group's ponies. They called the others to look at them.

After Nancy had examined the marks she commented, "These weren't made by our ponies. They're too faint and indistinct. They must have been here for a while and been partially obliterated by rain or dust."

"We'll follow them," Pop decided. "They may be a clue."

He asked Nancy to lead off, saying, "You have a detective's eye. If these prints lead somewhere, you'll be the one to find the place. I'm convinced of that."

Nancy blushed a little at the compliment. "I'm

sure all you ranchers could do the same thing," she said, smiling. "And as for Bess and George, I think you'll find them pretty good detectives in their own right."

All of them laughed and made a little bow, then saddled their horses and rode off at a brisk clip.

Though a little hard to follow, there were still enough footprints intact to lead the group to a hill not far away. It had a rocky slope.

Conversation had ceased and it seemed as if there was not a sound except the plodding of the walking ponies.

Suddenly Nancy reined in sharply. "Listen!" she called out.

The others pulled up abruptly and remained silent. Somewhere off in the distance they could hear a faint whinny.

"Could that be Ben Rall's pony?" Range asked.

"I hope so!" Bess said in a rising tone. "If Ben's there, we ought to punish him for rolling that tree down the hillside at us."

Pop Hamilton had another idea. He urged his mount to get closer to the sound. The others raced after him. A few minutes later he stopped her and asked the young people to listen. The whinny was definitely louder.

"That sounds like Major!" he said, excited.

Guided by the whinnies that finally became almost frantic, the group was led to a natural stone stable. Everyone dismounted and rushed inside.

There stood the stolen palomino!

The animal began to prance around, although he could not get loose. A heavy chain had been attached to his halter and then secured to a spike set deep into the rock.

"Major!" Pop exclaimed.

Bess rushed up and said, "Major, you poor fellow! I hope you haven't been mistreated!"

Again and again the beautiful pony nuzzled Pop. It seemed as if he could not get enough affection from the master he loved. Each of the girls and the two cowboys went up to pat Major. Aside from looking a little thin, the animal seemed to be in good condition.

"Now we can start for home," Pop said, beaming happily.

"Aren't we going to try to find the thief?" Nancy asked.

The rancher said he thought that would be like hunting for a needle in a haystack. "Most likely the culprit saw or heard us coming and hurried away from here."

The young detective and her friends did not agree. One by one they gave Pop reasons why the thief might be hiding in the area—in a cave, perhaps.

George said, "Unless he has another pony, how could he get away from here?"

"Maybe," said Bess, "if Ben Rall is the thief, he's off riding his own pony."

Pop listened to all the arguments, then said to Nancy, "Let's have your opinion of the whole thing."

"I'm beginning to think it was not Ben Rall who stole Major," she replied. "It's possible that whoever did it is connected in some way with Roger Paine's plane. There's a shortcut from here to the spot where we found the craft. Whenever the person piloting it arrives, he may walk over here and use Major for some kind of work—perhaps to carry heavy packages."

"What in the world could he be bringing out here?" Bess asked. "And why would he go to so much trouble to make deliveries?"

"He would if it's contraband," Nancy replied.

Range said, "Maybe the man is taking something important away from here."

"Like what?" George asked.

Range grinned. "Gold!"

Chuck laughed. "If there's any of that around, I'm going to start digging myself!"

Nancy reminded the others that they had come out to this area for three reasons: to find Major, to catch the horse thief, and to locate Roger Paine.

"I have a suggestion," she said. "Pop, would you please let me ride Major?"

"Sure. Why?"

"I'll give him his head and see if he'll lead me to the horse thief."

The rancher nodded his assent. They found

the pony's bridle hanging on another spike. After removing the halter, they slipped the bridle over his head. The saddle and saddle blanket lay on a protruding stone. When everything was adjusted, Nancy jumped astride the pony's back and urged him out of the rocky stable.

"Go find the thief!" she told the palomino. "Good boy! Then go find Roger Paine!"

Major lifted his ears and looked wise, as if he understood every word. The pony, finding that he was not being directed, turned at once in the direction of the Hamilton Ranch. Everyone laughed as Nancy guided Major back to the group.

She patted his neck. "We'll go home in a little while," she said. "Right now we have a job to do. Find the man who took you away from the ranch."

Once more the pony's ears stood straight up. Hopefully, Nancy waited. Once more Major veered around and headed for the ranch.

"I guess it's no use," the girl admitted and slid off the animal's back.

"This hill may have other hiding places," she told Pop Hamilton. Then she asked in a persuasive tone, "Shall we scout for some?"

This time Pop shook his head and said firmly, "The boys and I are needed at the ranch. It will be an overnight trip from here. That is all the time we can spare."

Pop rode his beloved Major, leading his other mount. They traveled until dark, then set up camp. Range rustled up a quick but substantial supper. As soon as they finished, everyone in the group crawled into his sleeping bag.

Sometime in the middle of the night all were awakened by shrill whinnies from the ponies. Somebody or something had spooked them!

As the travelers unzipped their sleeping bags and stood up, they suddenly froze. A shot had rung out!

CHAPTER VIII

Good-by, Speed Boy!

THE CAMPERS quickly stepped out of their sleeping bags and grabbed flashlights. They beamed them directly on the ponies.

The animals were rearing, snorting, and trying to break away from the tethers. Their upper lips were lifted angrily, and now and then one of them would whinny pathetically.

One pony lay on the ground. Had it been wounded? Killed? The girls did not dare go near it to find out since the animals were so agitated.

Pop and the boys, however, were trying their best to reassure the ponies with their presence. They talked to them and held the frightened animals tightly by their halters.

The three girls could do nothing but aim their flashlights around, hoping to get a glimpse of the person who had disturbed the ponies and fired the shot. For a fraction of a second Nancy caught sight of a man on the far side of the maddened ponies. He wore a kerchief up to his eyes and had a sombrero pulled low. There was no chance of identifying him.

Nancy screamed to Pop and his cowboys, nevertheless, "Over there!" She pointed to the place where she had seen the stranger.

She ran around the ring of animals and was just in time to see the intruder yank one of the ponies from the group and start to run off with it.

"Stop!" she cried.

Bess and George, who had followed her, took up the cry. Instead of pausing, the man dashed ahead a few yards, jumped onto the pony's back, and took off at breakneck speed. As long as he stayed within the beams of their flashlights, they could see him slapping the pony's flank hard to make him go even faster.

By this time Range had jumped onto his own horse and gone in pursuit of the thief, urging the animal to race as fast as he could.

George did not often show her emotions, but now she was very grim. "Oh, I hope nothing happens to Range!" she said. "This is such rough territory to be riding through in the dark. Besides, that man has a gun in a holster, I saw it. He won't mind using it!"

Nancy patted her friend on the shoulder. "I think Range knows what he's doing," she said. "Please don't worry."

The girls walked back to where the other ponies were gradually quieting down. Chuck had managed to calm them.

"Good work," Bess called out from the sidelines.

Chuck smiled, then hurried off to join Pop Hamilton, who was down on his knees examining the pony that had been shot.

The rancher shook his head sadly. "This is Speed Boy, the pony I rode out here. He was a gentleman and a faithful animal to his duties.

"Speed Boy, I'm sorry you cannot return to the ranch with us, but that villain made an accurate shot and has punctured your leg muscles so you could never walk again."

Bess Marvin could stand no more. She turned and walked off, but Nancy and George waited to hear the full eulogy.

"If there is a horse heaven," Pop went on, "you will be a fine addition to it. Good-by, Speed Boy, good-by!"

Nancy, George, and Chuck said together, "Good-by, Speed Boy!"

The three of them closed their eyes as the rancher used one shot to put the suffering pony out of his misery. Then the girls started to walk back to their camp, tears stinging their cheeks.

"It's terribly sad and so unnecessary," Nancy said. "But I suppose for Pop it would have been even worse if the thief had shot Major."

Pop and Chuck dug a grave for the animal and buried it, tears in their eyes also. One of the live ponies whinnied.

In the distance they could hear hoofbeats. A short time later Range rejoined his group. Alongside him was the stolen pony!

"Oh, you got him back!" Nancy exclaimed. "I'm so glad. How did you do it?"

Range explained that his horse was just on the verge of overtaking the thief when he jumped off and raced toward another man, who was astride one horse and holding another.

"The thief jumped on and sped off," Range concluded. "I thought the best thing to do was to bring our pony back here."

"Thanks so much," George said to him. The animal was the one she had been riding. "You really had us worried when you took off in the dark alone."

The cowboy grinned. "I'm used to night riding," he said. "There's nothing more exhilarating than being astride a horse in the moonlight."

He might have said more in a jocular vein, but just then Pop and Chuck walked up. Suddenly it occurred to Range that the girls' faces were tear-stained, Pop and Chuck looked somber, and none of them responded to his lightheartedness.

"What happened?" he asked.

When he heard about Speed Boy, Range, too, became sad. "He was a fine pony. This will be a big loss to the Hamilton Ranch. I'm sorry, Pop."

"Thank you," said the rancher. "Also for getting George's pony back. And now I think we should all head for bed."

Bess spoke. "Aren't you afraid the thief may return?"

"I doubt it," Pop replied. "I think he shot Speed Boy because the pony attacked him. He won't try any more thievery."

Range was not so sure of this. He repeated what had happened as he had approached the thief. "So he has not only his one pony, but a companion who also had a mount. The two of them may decide to come back together."

"Oh, no!" Bess cried out. "You mustn't let them! They might shoot another one of our ponies!"

They persuaded Pop to set up a watch for the remainder of the night.

"It will not be many hours until daybreak," he said. "We would leave before then. You young folks go to sleep, and I'll keep my eye open for that ornery thief."

Chuck and Range would not hear of this arrangement. "We'll take turns, same as we did before," Range said.

The ranch owner was adamant. He said, "As soon as we get to the ranch, you boys will have to get to work. Me, now—" he smiled a little—"I can take a rest. You get yours now."

There was no more conversation, and soon everyone except Pop and Nancy was sound asleep. Nancy snuggled into her sleeping bag, but lay staring up at the sky. She wished she had been able to get a better look at the thief. Who was he? Just a wanderer who stole horses whenever he had a chance?

The girl detective put this thought out of her mind. "I have a strong hunch," she told herself, "that he's after bigger stakes than stealing horses. Somehow or other he's connected with the mystery I'm trying to solve. Oh well, maybe someday I'll find out."

She turned over and dozed off. When Pop's cheerful whistle came to awaken the camp, it seemed to her that dawn had arrived very soon. All the girls were bleary-eyed, since they were not used to such early rising hours. The ride to the ranch in the invigorating, clear morning air thoroughly awakened them, however. In a little over three hours they reached the Hamilton Ranch, where an appetizing breakfast awaited them.

Bess asked Nancy afterwards if she had made any plans for the girls that day. The young detective shook her head. "I thought I'd work on this silver medal and try to decipher the strange figures on it."

Bess and George were eager to help. All three girls copied the symbols on pieces of paper and then tried to figure out their meaning.

After twenty minutes had gone by with no re-sults, Nancy suddenly snapped her fingers.

"I just thought of something!" she said. "One of the detective books I was reading had a chapter on handwriting. I recall that in one place it said that the lowest part of the letters in any word or sentence is extremely difficult to figure out.

"Possibly these queer-looking marks are the bottoms of letters. Let's see what we can make out of them."

Once more the three girls went to work. They covered several sheets of paper, trying to evolve full letters out of the symbols. Again there was complete silence for a long time.

Then suddenly Bess cried out, excited, "I think the second and third words are—'bomb site'!"

CHAPTER IX

Magnetic Cloud

"BOMB SITE?" Nancy repeated. "It doesn't mean anything to me. Where? What?"

"I know what it means to me," Bess exclaimed fearfully. "We might be blown sky high!"

She insisted on telling Pop Hamilton about this at once, and rushed off.

Nancy and George were not frightened. The message did not indicate the bomb site was local. The girls continued to work on the puzzling message.

A few minutes later Nancy said, "I have the word before 'bomb site.' "

"What is it?" George asked.

"Revolution!" the young detective replied.

George was stunned. "You're right. I got as far as 'rev,' Nancy. The mystery is getting deeper."

Bess returned, saying she could not find Pop

Hamilton. She was shocked when she heard the word "revolution."

"Maybe we shouldn't stay here," she said.

Nancy suggested that they all hunt for Pop, perhaps on horseback. The three girls searched for him, but could not locate the rancher. They finally concluded that he had ridden far out on the range.

"I guess we'll have to wait until tonight," Bess said. "But I admit I'm scared silly."

A few minutes later Chuck rode in. He greeted the girls, said he had come only to pick up some tools, and was going right back to where the boys were working.

"We're mending a fence," he told them. Then, looking at Bess, he asked, "How about your getting a pony and riding up there with me?"

The girl's mood changed completely. In the wink of an eye she had forgotten her discovery and the worry about the words "revolution" and "bomb site."

She ran back to the ranch house to change her riding pants, which she had torn, and was ready by the time Chuck finished his errand. The two rode off, laughing.

Nancy and George looked at each other and grinned. They would have to continue to decipher the words on the back of the medal without Bess's assistance!

The two girls continued to puzzle over the rest of the strange symbols, which they believed were also parts of words. They assumed that the balance of the message followed the same pattern—each symbol was the lowest quarter of a letter. There was total silence in the room as Nancy and George used more sheets of scratch paper trying to figure out other words from the marks etched into the medal. Finally Nancy did find one.

"The word below 'bomb site' is 'under,'" she stated.

"Good," said George. "But 'under' what? Now the whole thing is becoming very complicated. Where is the revolution bomb site?"

Nancy happened to glance out of the window. The men were just coming in from their work. Chuck and Bess trailed behind. Pop had already turned his pony over to Pete and was heading toward the ranch house.

"Now's our chance to talk to him," Nancy said. "Come on!"

The two girls hurried outside and met Pop as he walked to the house.

Nancy asked, "Did you talk to Bess?"

The rancher shook his head. "Is there any reason why I should have?"

Nancy told him about the words "revolution, bomb site," and "under" on the back of the silver medal. Pop listened politely, but shrugged off the

George was stunned. "The mystery is getting deeper!" she said.

idea that the medal and message had anything to do with the area near Hamilton Ranch.

"There's absolutely nothing around here to bomb, and not enough people to start a revolution," he said. "The strange message must refer to some other locale."

Nancy and George had to admit that there was logic in what he said, but as they walked off, both of them felt he might be wrong. Why had the medal been dropped in this area, perhaps by the person flying Roger Paine's plane?

"I only hope," said George, "that the bomb site is a good distance away from the Hamilton Ranch."

"And the Excello Flying School," Nancy added.

Both girls believed that if they could decipher more of the strange symbols on the medal, they would be able to pinpoint the exact location.

The three girls had no time to work on the puzzle the following morning. Bess and George had horseback-riding dates, and Nancy was to take a flying lesson.

She met Bruce on schedule and soon was in the pilot's seat of the Excello craft. As she raced down the runway for a takeoff, the girl detective asked, "Okay if we aim for the mystery spot, Bruce?"

He grinned. "You don't give up easily, do you? But I admit I'm just as anxious as you to see the kidnapping case solved. So go ahead."

As they approached the area where the big cloud was, they spotted an oncoming plane.

Bruce said, "Roger's craft is equipped with a radio that can be tuned to UNICOM. I'll see if I can raise him."

He turned to a frequency of 122.8 megacycles. There was no response to his call, but the plane was getting closer.

"You'd better climb!" Bruce said.

Nancy pulled gently on the stick and climbed a hundred feet above the path of the oncoming plane. She asked Bruce to look through the binoculars to see if he could identify the other craft.

He did so and exclaimed, "That's Roger's plane all right! But I can't understand why it doesn't answer me!"

Nancy replied, "If the mysterious sky phantom is the pilot, he won't answer you!"

The stranger began a wide turn, which took him to the far side of the big cloud.

Nancy also banked and turned for a chase. As they came near the cloud, she and Bruce were just in time to see Paine's plane disappear inside the mysterious formation.

"Now what are we going to do?" Nancy asked. "Just keep going round and round until whoever is in there is forced out or pleads for help?"

The flying instructor did not reply at once. At last he said, "Roger's plane is larger than this one and has more fuel capacity. We'd probably run out of gas before he would. Perhaps we should land near the spot where he leaves his plane and watch."

Before Nancy had a chance to figure out her approach pattern, she encountered a strong tailwind and turbulence that forced her directly underneath the cloud.

The next moment there was a terrific updraft. It carried her plane into the vapory mass!

"Oh!" Nancy cried out, bewildered. "Bruce, quick! Take the controls!"

He did so, but just avoided a collision with Roger Paine's craft, which shot out of the cloud. It quickly rose above the turbulence and went off. Bruce followed the same procedure, but did not attempt to chase the other plane.

When Nancy's heart stopped thumping, she said, "Can we go back inside the big cloud and see if we can pick up a clue to why the sky phantom hid in there? Evidently it's not so dangerous as people say."

Bruce nodded. He turned again and flew directly into the cloud. They went round the edges of the vapory mass and down to the center. There was nothing to be seen.

"I guess it's just a hiding place for the sky phantom," Bruce said and made another turn, going into a different section of the giant cloud.

Suddenly, dead ahead, they came face to face

with a strange sight. The dark outline of a giant!
The face was grizzly looking and indistinct.

"What is it?" Nancy asked, wondering if this
was some great creature that might attack them.
Bruce passed it and laughed at Nancy's fear.

"Would you like Sir Galahad Bruce Fisher to
run him through?" he asked.

The remark made Nancy grin. She imagined
the young pilot wearing a medieval coat of armor
with pilot wings on the breastplate. Without
hesitation she said, "Yes, Sir Galahad, run him
through!"

Turning, Bruce approached the dark, menac-
ing giant and whipped down the center of it. Now
the pilot came out of the great cloud.

"Had enough excitement?" he asked his pupil,
who was staring ahead, unable to believe what she
had just seen.

Nancy shook her head. "Please, Bruce, let's go
back inside the cloud and see if the black giant
disappeared. What was it, anyway?"

Bruce said it was a midget storm cloud held in
place by the larger white formation. The oblig-
ing teacher went down under the cloud and again
swooped up into it.

To his and Nancy's amazement, the storm
cloud had reassembled. Now it looked like an in-
furiated lion ready to attack!

"This is an interesting phenomenon," Bruce

remarked. "I believe the storm cloud is made of infinitesimal bits of magnetic particles."

Wondering what form the black vapory mass might take next, Nancy decided they should pierce it and find out.

"Okay, my lady, your wish is my command," Bruce said with a twinkle in his eyes. "Here we go!"

Nancy grinned, but a few seconds later her face froze. Suddenly, on his approach to the inner cloud, all the instruments in the plane went haywire! Next the lights blotted out.

Nancy and Bruce were in complete darkness with no reliable means of navigation!

CHAPTER X

Awkward Situation

'ALTHOUGH Bruce and Nancy knew they were in a precarious spot, he remained calm and she did not panic.

She sat quietly, clutching the sides of the pilot's seat. Bruce was trying his best to keep the plane straight and level. Not only were his maneuvers useless, but it seemed as if the craft were being sucked into the magnetic cloud.

The plane was wobbling badly, making a forward and backward rocking motion. Nancy began to feel a little squeamish.

"We must get out of here!" Bruce said, his jaw set grimly.

"Is there anything I can do to help?" Nancy asked presently.

He did not reply for several seconds. Then he said, "Yes, I want you to work on something. You take the stick and follow my directions while I try to find out what's wrong with our flight instruments and the lights."

"Okay."

"Try to keep her straight and level!" he said.

Nancy did her best, but the magnetic influence from the inner cloud continued to toss the plane about like a balloon.

Two dreadful thoughts came to the young sleuth's mind. Had the sky phantom deliberately lured them into the great cloud with the thought of causing them to crash? Or was it possible that they would remain prisoners of the magnetic mass until they died? The latter possibility made her wince, but she kept her mind on what she was doing

Nancy tried to remain at the same speed and stay straight and level. She seemed to be standing still alongside the black formation.

"Anyway, that's better than falling out of the sky," she thought, trying to keep up her own spirits.

Meanwhile, Bruce frantically tapped the instrument panel with his fist in an effort to unstick the indicator needles.

"Any luck?" Nancy asked.

"No," Bruce replied.

"I'm beginning to lose control of the plane!" the girl detective warned. "You'd better take over and do it fast!"

"Try to hold on for just a bit longer," Bruce

pleaded. "I have an idea. Most of our instruments are electrically operated. The magnetic force of this cloud must be interfering with the circuitry."

"What can we do?" Nancy asked.

"A couple of our flight-altitude instruments have an alternate source for operation," the apparently calm instructor declared. "It works on a vacuum system rather than an electric one."

Bruce leaned forward and located the selector switch. He quickly turned it clockwise to where the selector dial was marked "vacuum."

Nancy watched the panel with relief as the gyro compass and artificial horizon suddenly came to life and then stabilized. A second later her instructor took over the controls.

"We're out of the cloud!" Nancy cried gleefully. "To tell you the truth, Bruce, I was never more frightened in my life! I really thought this would be the end for both of us."

Her teacher looked at the girl and said, "One thing you must never do in a plane when you're in a tight spot is to panic. Instead, assume that you are master of the situation and that you'll get out of your predicament all right."

Nancy nodded. "I'll try to remember that, but you have to admit this was really scary."

"Yes," Bruce conceded, "but during the years you'll be flying you'll be in many ticklish situations. You must be ready for every one as it comes along."

As they flew toward the Excello School, Nancy wondered whether or not she had actually learned more about flying or about the attitude one should have in order to be a good pilot.

After she taxied to the main building to report on her lesson, Nancy told everyone about the magnetic black cloud inside the great white one. Everybody standing around was amazed to hear of the vapory giant and lion that had nearly devoured the pair.

One of the pilots chuckled and said, "It sounds like a fairy tale."

"But it's true!" Nancy said.

Others in the room began to tease Bruce and his pupil, admitting that they thought the couple were trying to spoof them.

An Indian mechanic at the field, who had been seated in a corner of the room, now got up from his chair and walked forward.

"Bruce is telling the truth," he said. "My grandfather said that the big cloud is bewitched. Sometimes fire shoots out of it!"

All eyes turned in the Indian's direction. The pilots agreed that perhaps there was something to the story after all!

Nancy asked him, "Was this due to a sudden lightning storm?"

The Indian said he did not know. "I think not," he replied. "If this had been so, I believe my grandfather would have told us that. He was a student of the stars and of storms."

As soon as Nancy and Bruce had filed their report, he drove her to the ranch. Pop Hamilton and some of the cowboys standing around listened with interest to Nancy's story, but none of them believed it.

Chuck said, smiling, "You should have brought us a souvenir!"

The girl sleuth said, "Next time," and went to her room. In a few minutes Bess and George came in.

When Nancy described her adventure, Bess shivered. "What an awful experience!" she said. "Didn't you just about die?"

Nancy admitted that for a few minutes she had thought she and Bruce were finished. "It's a horrible feeling."

George spoke up. "You'd better not let your Dad hear about this," she advised. "He might forbid you to take any more flying lessons with Bruce, even if he is an expert."

Nancy did not reply, and Bess changed the subject. "Have you heard about the great party that's planned for tonight?"

"No," Nancy said.

"There's to be a masquerade," Bess went on. "They just decided on it."

Nancy glanced at her watch. "They haven't

given us much time to think of costumes. I'm afraid my wardrobe is a bit meager to try doing something original with it."

There was silence for a while as the girls searched for both clothes and inspiration.

At last Bess had an idea. "I'll go as a gypsy," she decided. With a giggle she added, "I'll borrow the bedspread from my cot for a gown, and take two rings from the drapery pole to hang over my ears. And I'll use my own bracelets."

George left the room and returned in a little while with a pair of cowboy boots three times too big for her.

"This is the first part of my clown costume," she announced. "I think Pop will lend me his big red shirt. "I'll let the long sleeves hang down and cover my hands completely." The usually conservative girl said she would fix up her face with rouge and powder to complete the outfit.

The other girls laughed, and Nancy said, "You'll look great. I'm going to wear this long white dress, or nightgown, whichever you want to call it, and borrow some white cheesecloth to wind around and around me."

"Are you trying to be the great white cloud?" George teased.

"That's not a bad idea," Nancy answered. "Actually I thought I'd call myself the blithe spirit, but maybe strange cloud would be better."

There was still an hour before suppertime, so

again the three girls sat down to decode the balance of the symbols engraved into the medal.

After a little while George called out, "I have one!"

"What is it?" Nancy asked eagerly.

George replied, "We know the first word on the second line is 'under.' I have the next one. I think the word is 'great.' "

The other girls were excited. "Now we're getting someplace," Nancy said.

Just then the telephone rang. She was next to it, so she picked up the instrument.

"It's Ned!" Nancy exclaimed, "and Burt, and also Dave—— Come and listen!"

The three girls crowded together as Ned said, "We have a surprise for you girls. We'll be out very soon to visit!"

"How soon?" Nancy asked.

"Any day now," Ned replied.

"Hi!" came Burt's voice. "We can't wait to see you girls."

George said that the ranch was a great place for a good time and she would be glad to see them. "I'll show you all around."

"Hi, Bess!" Dave called into the phone. "How is everything?"

When Bess did not answer immediately, he asked, "Are you there, Bess? And are you all right? I'm counting the hours until I see you!"

Bess mumbled into the phone, saying "Yes.

Here I am. I'm fine. B-bring your r-riding clothes!" she stuttered.

Ned came back on. "Can't talk any longer. Our three minutes are over. He hung up, and so did Nancy. She and George turned to look at Bess. Why had she stuttered on the phone?

"What's the matter with you?" her cousin asked.

Bess was very pale. "What am I going to do about Chuck?" she murmured.

George said abruptly, "You shouldn't have been so super nice to him. He thinks now that you're in love with him!"

"Maybe I am!" Bess said and burst into tears.

CHAPTER XI

Masked Intruder

Bess flopped on her cot and buried her face in the pillow. She sobbed convulsively.

Nancy sat down on the edge of the cot and patted Bess's back. "Be honest with George and me," she said. "Are you more fond of Chuck than you are of Dave?"

"I don't know! I don't know!" Bess mumbled in reply.

George, who tended to be less gentle with Bess than Nancy was, said tartly, "Get hold of yourself! You're old enough to make up your mind."

Bess turned over and looked at the other two girls with sad eyes. "You simply don't understand, George."

"I admit that," her cousin agreed. "You're acting like a big cry baby."

Bess tried to defend herself. "How would you act if Range should ask you to marry him and stay out here to live, as Chuck asked me?"

The question and disclosure were so surprising that George was taken off guard. She stopped chastising her cousin but refused to answer the question.

"I'm going outdoors," she said abruptly and left the room.

Nancy began to stroke Bess's hair. "Why don't you wait," she said, "until Dave and the others get here? Then you can compare them. Offhand, I'd say both are fine boys. Dave has eastern ways, and Chuck has a western outlook. You have to make up your mind which appeals to you more."

Bess looked at Nancy gratefully. "You always seem to know the right way to decide everything," she said. "You've helped a lot. I feel much better."

Nancy stood up and smiled. "I hope your remark about my decisions will apply to this mystery we're trying to solve. We've had so many false leads it seems to me we're not making much headway."

"But you'll do it," Bess said reassuringly. "I wish I had your will power."

Nancy was embarrassed and said she was going outside too for a little while.

"I'm so sorry you have this problem, Bess. Probably you should be alone to think. Why don't you take a shower and a shampoo? I'm sure it'll make you feel better," Nancy suggested. "When George and I come back, we'll all go to dinner."

As Nancy reached the ranch-house lobby, she was hailed by the desk clerk. "If you and your friends don't have your masks for tonight, you're to go to Pop's office and get them as soon as possible." he said. "The pretty ones are being chosen fast."

Nancy thanked him and went to the rancher's private office. Several guests were there, trying on various types of masks. Most of them covered just the eyes and nose, but there were a few that hid the whole face.

Nancy chose a half mask, thinking it would go well with her filmy white costume. Then she picked out a dark tan mask, which she felt would be appropriate for Bess's gypsy outfit. Perhaps she would tell fortunes.

"George has already been here," Pop said, "and chosen hers."

When Nancy returned to the room a little while later, Bess was asleep. George had not returned but she came in soon. She had picked up a red mask to go with her clown costume. She put it on.

Bess awoke with a start. "Oh!" she exclaimed.

"Feeling better?" George asked.

Her cousin looked around the room wildly. "Oh, I had the most horrible dream!" she said. "Dave and Chuck were having a duel!"

George laughed. "They probably will do just that after Dave gets here."

"Don't say that!" Bess cried out. "In my dream they killed each other!"

"Hypers! You sure are letting your imagination run away with you," George commented. "You'd better get up and dress for dinner. Remember, tonight is the masquerade."

Nancy had made no comment about Bess's dream, but she was a little concerned about how Dave would view the situation when he arrived. She fervently hoped there would be no real trouble between the two boys, who did not yet know they were rivals.

The three girls put on dresses and were soon joining the other guests who were walking to the dining room. Streamers festooned the ceiling, and pictures of Hamilton Ranch ponies, past and present, hung on the walls. To each one had been attached a bow and long, hanging ribbons in various colors.

The girls walked around quickly to look at them, wondering if Speed Boy's photograph might be there, and if so, what color ribbon would be on it. They could not find it.

"I thought for sure Speed Boy would be here," Nancy said.

A waitress, overhearing her remark, said, "Pop took the picture away. He told us it would have to have a black ribbon, and he thought no note of sadness should be displayed at the party tonight."

"Thank you," Nancy said.

She and her friends went to their table and found party menus awaiting them. The whole dinner was a gala one, and an excellent preparation for the dance, which would commence in about two hours.

"It ought to be fun," George declared.

After dinner, the girls went to their room to change into the costumes they planned to wear. When they arrived at the dining-room door, the trio found that all the tables had been removed. Chairs lined the walls and an open double door at one side of the room led to a garden beyond. A band was playing a lively march.

"The parade is about to start," Pop warned, and the girls hurried to get in line. There was loud applause as they passed various groups of watchers. After everyone had walked all the way around the room, the march ended and the dance music started. Chuck had recognized Bess and immediately claimed her as a partner. Range was on hand to ask George.

She looked at him in surprise. "How did you manage to spot me so quickly?" she asked.

He grinned as they danced off. "Who else but you would think of being a lady clown? You look great!"

At the same moment Nancy was claimed by a stranger wearing a sailor's work clothes and a full face mask.

"You sure look mighty purty tonight," he said.

Nancy thought his voice sounded familiar, but she could not identify it.

"Do I know you?" Nancy inquired.

"I don't guess you do, but let's dance."

Nancy was puzzled. It always bothered her when she could not recognize a voice at once.

The stranger swept her around the room in long strides, but stopped abruptly at the door that led to the garden.

"It's too bloomin' hot in here," he said. "Come on outside."

Nancy did not trust the man. She suddenly recalled the time she had been kidnapped from a masquerade party at her friend Ned Nickerson's fraternity house.

"I'd rather not," she said.

"Aw, come on!" the man said.

He began yanking her by the hand. When he could not budge Nancy, the stranger put an arm around her shoulders and pushed her toward the doorway.

This was enough for Nancy. With a quick jerk, she removed his mask!

"Ben Rall!" she cried out. "You don't work here any more. You weren't invited to this party."

"Never mind that, you little tartar. You're going to come with me!"

"I am not!" Nancy shouted at the top of her voice. "Let me alone!"

Other dancers, hearing the argument, rushed to

the girl's side. The men hustled the unwanted, obnoxious Ben outdoors and Nancy heard one of them say, "Get away from here and stay away! You understand? You don't belong here!"

The men's partners gathered around Nancy. One of them said, "I'm glad you got rid of that pest!"

At this moment another man came up. Though he wore a half mask, Nancy immediately recognized the man dressed in a soldier's uniform.

"Bruce!" she cried out. "Am I glad to see you!"

He led her onto the dance floor and said, "I guess I got here just in the nick of time, and I suppose you're surprised to see me. Pop Hamilton invited several of the instructors at Excello to come to the party."

Nancy said she was happy to hear this. When the music stopped, Bruce remarked, "It's warm in here. Would you mind walking outside with me?"

"Of course not," Nancy replied.

Bruce said, "I'd like to talk to you about tomorrow morning's flying lesson. Also, I wanted to tell you that the school telephoned Roger Paine's home again. His parents still have not heard from him, and I think they're getting the FBI to make a search. So you may have company in your sleuthing."

Nancy said she thought the Paines were certainly doing the right thing. "As you know, I suspected foul play from the start," she added.

Bruce asked if she had had any new hunches. "Most of yours turn out to be correct guesses."

Nancy thanked him for the compliment, then said she would never forget the amazing experience of flying inside the big cloud, with the fantastic magnetic black formation.

"That giant was like a sky phantom," she said. "He could change shape whenever anything disturbed him."

Suddenly she realized that Bruce was not listening attentively. She looked sideways at him.

He apologized. "I was just thinking about something I'd like to do tomorrow in our lesson," he said. "We'll try a new spot, where the winds and terrain are different from any place where we have been."

"That sounds interesting," said Nancy. "I'll be on time."

Bruce looked at her intently. "I have a surprise for you, but it will have to wait until tomorrow. Yes, the secret will have to wait until tomorrow."

CHAPTER XII

Breaking the Code

DURING the evening, Nancy speculated on the secret that Bruce declined to tell her. She tried several ways to get him to divulge it, but failed. The pilot merely grinned and refused to commit himself.

The next morning he arrived early in his car and the two drove to the Excello Flying School. Bruce's plane was ready, so he and his pupil climbed aboard.

"Do you want me to take the controls?" Nancy asked him.

"I certainly do," Bruce said. "Well, I'll tell you where we're going. That's the secret." He grinned. "I can have my mysteries too. We're flying to an entirely different location this time—in fact, one that is flat and reasonably smooth. If we come down, taxiing won't be so difficult. But before we do that, I'm going to teach you something about accidental spins."

Nancy gasped at the thought of possibly spinning right down to the ground, but she said nothing to Bruce.

In about half an hour, they reached the practice area. "Ready?" Bruce asked.

"Quite," Nancy replied.

Bruce rolled into a steep turn. "Do you remember how you accidentally spun over the top during a previous lesson?" he asked.

"How could I forget?" Nancy answered.

"I'm going to demonstrate a similar situation to you," the instructor declared. "However, this time we'll spin *out of the bottom* of the turn, rather than *over the top*."

Nancy braced herself as Bruce tightened the turn to the left. Then suddenly he pulled the stick back with a snap and shoved the left rudder pedal forward. A split second later the plane whipped into a vicious spin.

Nancy grabbed the sides of her pilot's seat. "Oh!" she murmured.

After several turns Bruce recovered from the maneuver.

"Whew!" Nancy sighed. "What a ride!"

"Rough, isn't it?" Bruce said, "but I want to be certain that you fully understand these maneuvers so you won't get into trouble in the future."

"May I try one?" the girl flier asked nervously. Then she told herself she must be calm.

Guided by her instructor, Nancy manipulated

the controls. Her first attempt merely resulted in a tight spiral, but her second and third tries yielded excellent spins.

"Very good," Bruce commented.

Nancy, herself, was pleased. After half an hour of practice, however, the girl flier confessed that she was beginning to feel a bit dizzy. "I've had enough."

Bruce grinned. "I imagine you'd like to go down to terra firma for a while."

Nancy would not admit that her pulse was still racing even though she had done the last maneuver very well.

"Yes, let's."

They had no sooner touched down and Nancy cut off the engine than Bruce lay down and put his ear to the ground. Nancy watched, wondering why he was doing this.

"Someone's riding near here," he announced a moment later.

While the couple waited, Nancy hoped fervently that the oncoming horseman would not be Ben Rall. She mentioned this to Bruce, who frowned.

"I hope not also, because I'd sure be tempted to punch him!"

It turned out that the rider was not Ben Rall. He was a stranger to Nancy and Bruce, who introduced himself as John Wade. He did not wait for them to tell him their names.

"You folks out for a little jaunt?" he asked pleasantly. He was a sun-tanned, medium-sized, rather stout man, who patted his tummy affectionately. "When I saw you coming down, I thought I'd give Susie gal here a break. She can rest while I talk to you."

Wade dismounted and looked at the plane. "Pretty neat little job," he remarked. "I sometimes use a small craft in my work. But today I felt like getting away alone and chose to ride the pony."

The man explained that he was an oil prospector. "There's probably no oil here, but then, one never knows."

Nancy introduced herself and Bruce, then asked John Wade, "Do you live nearby?"

"Oh, no," he replied. "I live a long way off. But I flew to a ranch some miles from this territory and borrowed this pony. There's an old superstition that a man's horse will lead him to gold. Maybe this one will find some black gold for me."

He looked at Nancy. Then, as if she did not understand what he was saying, he added, "Black gold is a nickname for oil."

Nancy's detective instincts were aroused. "You must have some kind of information or clue that there is oil in this area," she said, and waited eagerly for him to answer.

The prospector laughed. "Yes, I had a tip. I haven't much hope that it means a thing, but if there's any sign at all, I want to try out a new invention of mine. I've always thought it was a shame that when men drill for oil a gusher sometimes comes in that can't be stopped. A lot of oil is wasted before the well can be capped. I hope to change that.

"With my invention there won't be any wasted oil. Right now one of my gadgets is tied onto my pony. The device drills a tiny hole, so a small stream of oil can flow out with very little lost."

"That sounds great," Bruce remarked. "I'd like to see it working."

John Wade proved to be a continuous and rather tiresome talker. Nancy found it easier to listen than to try thinking of something to say to the man. Presently his comments shifted back to the Excello Flying School plane Nancy and Bruce were using.

"She's really a little beauty," he said, gazing intently at the craft. Turning to Bruce he added, "Would you object if I climb aboard and look her over?"

Bruce winked at Nancy, then said to Mr. Wade, "Not at all. I'll join you."

As John Wade turned, Nancy smiled at the pilot. She had guessed what he was thinking. He did not want this stranger to disappear suddenly with his plane!

As the prospector went inside the cabin, Nancy began to wonder if there was any possibility that the man could be connected with Roger Paine's apparent abduction, or with the sky phantom. Maybe he was out reconnoitering and was not really an oil prospector at all!

"But I must be fair," she decided, and tried to erase this suspicious idea from her mind.

The man seemed to be very nice, and she did feel that he had an honest face. Nancy put any thought of trouble from her mind. She would take his word that he was a prospector and inventor.

While waiting for the two men to reappear, the girl detective sat down on the stubby grass. She pulled a copy of the cryptogrammatic message on the medal from her shirt pocket. With a pencil she tried to make whole letters from the small lowest part of the words yet to be deciphered. She became so absorbed in her project that she did not notice how much time had passed.

When she had nearly completed one word, Nancy hoped nobody would disturb her. The only sound she could hear was the rumble of the men's voices in the plane.

"This is it!" Nancy thought suddenly. The young sleuth was ecstatic! The last word in the puzzling code was "cloud." Now the whole cryptogram read:

REVOLUTION BOMB SITE
UNDER GREAT CLOUD

With no idea what the message meant, Nancy was

eager to get back to the ranch and share her find with Pop Hamilton, Bess, and George. She was sure this message called for immediate action.

Nancy glanced up at the doorway of the plane. The men were still conversing animatedly. She stood up, stretched, and gazed around. Suddenly her eyes focused on one spot. Mr. Wade's pony was no longer standing where he had left him!

The young detective turned in a complete circle, viewing the landscape in all directions as far as she could see. Finally she detected the animal running off in the distance. She was a mere speck with legs.

Nancy cried out loudly, "Bruce! Mr. Wade! The pony's gone!"

The girl's cry had rung out so loudly that both men appeared in the doorway at once. She repeated the bad news.

"Where is she?" Mr. Wade asked in concern.

Nancy pointed. "I think that's probably your pony way over there."

The prospector panicked. "We must get her back!" he yelled. "She's carrying all my special equipment, which must not fall into the hands of anyone else!" Turning to Bruce, he said, "Will you take me in your plane to capture her?"

The pilot looked skeptical. "Of course, I can taxi all the way down this valley, but it would be a rough ride. I can't go very fast, and your animal may disappear before I can reach that spot."

Mr. Wade would not take no for an answer.

"I've got to save my equipment!" he almost screamed. "No one must see my invention!"

Finally Bruce said, "Nancy would you mind staying here for a little while? I'll come back as quickly as I can. The plane will hold only two of us."

"I don't mind," she replied. "I may even look around a little."

After the plane had started its run, she gazed off to her right. Not far away she saw a hillside that was partly rocky and partly covered with vegetation.

"That seems like an unusual formation," she thought. "I think I'll go over and investigate that place."

Nancy crossed the flat area, then began walking along the foot of the hillside. By this time both the pony and the plane were out of sight.

Nancy's attention was suddenly directed toward a nearby opening in the hillside. Was there a cave beyond?

The opening was small, but large enough for her to squeeze through. Unhooking her flashlight from the belt of her jeans, she beamed it into the enclosed area ahead. To her surprise, the cave was apparently a large one.

"How exciting!" she thought. "I must see what's inside!"

CHAPTER XIII

Cave Mice

NANCY squeezed through the narrow opening to the cave, beaming her flashlight ahead of her. The interior was large but the ceiling was low. She could barely stand up straight.

As she progressed, the rough stones above her brushed against her hair, and she ducked often. There was nothing on the walls, ceiling, or floor of the cave to indicate that anyone lived in the place.

"Maybe the sky phantom uses this for a hideout," she thought.

A short distance ahead Nancy came to several stone steps, which led to a lower level. She stopped to examine them. Were they natural or had they been hewn out by some ancient Indians? They were very smooth and could have been worn by a lot of travel up and down.

"This might have been a ceremonial cave, where the Indians had their religious meetings," Nancy decided. The sandy earth floor seemed to have had fires on it for cooking with the ashes dispersed and trampled. There were no artifacts of any kind, however.

"Probably looters have taken everything away," Nancy thought.

She descended the steps and beamed her flashlight around. She looked for niches or corridors that might lead out of the cave. The air inside seemed to be fresh and Nancy thought she could feel a slight draft. She concluded there must be another opening.

The young sleuth kept walking. She could not see any side exits large enough for a man to get through.

Suddenly she gave a soft scream. Mice were appearing from everywhere. They scurried across the floor, up the steps, and back toward the entrance. There were hundreds of them!

"I must have scared those mice out of their hiding places," Nancy thought. She smiled to herself. "Well, I can get along without them. I'm glad they're going in the opposite direction and not bothering me."

At this instant she became aware of two other happenings. Larger mice were now appearing. They seemed to be coming out of the rocks! They, too, started to scoot past her. At the same time Nancy thought she felt rain. Was there a leak from the ceiling?

As she looked up, the girl explorer realized that this was not rain dropping down. It was oil!

"I'd better leave," she decided.

With mice all around her, she began to run toward the steps, but she could not get far. Already the oil shower was becoming heavier, making the floor very slippery.

Nancy slipped several times and fell twice. She did not seem to be able to make any headway.

"I must hurry out of here!" she thought frantically.

At last, by sliding to one side of the cave, she managed to pull herself along and finally get over to the steps. But now she found it impossible to mount them.

The oily rain had stopped abruptly but despite this Nancy found the stone steps too slippery to climb. After several attempts to get partway up and sliding back, she ceased to try this method of escape.

"I'm glad the rain stopped," she told herself, and beamed the flashlight around to see if there was any possible way to hold onto the wall and climb up. She found none.

Now Nancy glanced at her watch. She had been gone a long time. If Bruce and John Wade had returned, they would certainly wonder where she was.

"I *must* get out of here!" she resolved. The girl detective noticed that the oil seemed to be seeping into the sandy ground fairly rapidly. This gave her hope, even though she knew it would take a while for it to disappear entirely. In the meantime there might be another shower of oil!

Suddenly she smiled. "Those mice are a lot smarter than I am! They knew just when to get out of here. I wonder how soon they'll come back!"

Nancy concluded she could not wait to find out. She must think of another way to escape from this oil-slick cave.

"I have to tell John Wade about the oil," she thought. "It seems strange that there is no activity—no drilling—around here. Could it be possible that none of the natives have found out what's going on?"

An idea came to her. She took off her sweater and doubled it up. Using it as a mop, she partially dried off the stone steps and managed to get to the upper level. When she reached the top, it was easier to walk because the oil had seeped into the earth as if the ground were a sponge. Nancy felt sure the formation of this small hill must be stone and sand.

When she reached the opening and squeezed through, the girl detective looked off into the distance. Bruce's plane was back! Excited over her find of oil, she hurried forward to tell John Wade

Nancy slid and fell in the oily rain.

about it. When Nancy arrived, she looked around but did not see the prospector. Bruce was seated inside alone.

"Where's Mr. Wade?" she asked.

"After we found his pony, he rode off."

"You mean he isn't coming back?" Nancy queried.

By this time Bruce had climbed out of the plane and stood looking at the girl. Then he began to laugh. "No, John isn't coming back, but he'll wish he had. You're a sight, Nancy! What in the world happened to you?"

He continued to laugh so hard that Nancy began to look at her clothes and to feel her hair. She was covered with oil from head to toe!

"I guess you're right," she told the pilot. "Bruce, this is *oil!* I got a shower bath of it in a cave I found."

Bruce looked skeptical. "You what?"

Nancy told him the whole story and ended by saying the mice had had more sense than she about leaving before the oil shower. Bruce shook his head and burst into laughter again.

"I'm sure sorry I missed that scene," he said. "Well, hop aboard!"

"Not this way," Nancy replied. "I'll ruin the plane with all this icky stuff."

Bruce said he would soon fix that. He took the oily sweater from her hand and dropped it into a metal container on the plane. Then he pulled out a bag of cloth wipers for her to use. They were all colors of the rainbow and made from all kinds of materials. Nancy found that the rolls of cheese-cloth were the most effective.

Bruce helped sop the oil from her hair and back, then he got into the plane and covered the copilot's seat with a large piece of cloth. Finally he announced that he was ready for her to come aboard.

"I'd better do the flying," he said. "I think you've had enough adventures for one day."

As Nancy climbed in, she said, "Bruce, instead of going back to Excello, couldn't we fly in the direction John Wade took? I want so much to tell him about the oil I discovered."

The pilot agreed. He zoomed down the flat, scrubby field, then took off. First he flew over the spot where he had overtaken the runaway pony.

"John went on from here," he said. "I think in this direction."

He banked sharply. Without warning the engine quit. Bruce immediately lowered the nose of the craft to maintain flying speed. "We can't make a forced landing straight ahead!" he shouted. "The terrain's too rough."

"What'll we do?" Nancy gasped. "We haven't much altitude!"

Only the rush of the airstream could be heard in the cockpit. It was an ominous sound to the instructor and his student.

"Hold on!" Bruce cried. "I'm going to try something!"

The pilot's knowledge of the area was to come in handy. He made a shallow turn in a southeasterly course.

"The ground is coming up fast!" Nancy observed anxiously.

Bruce said nothing. He kept descending straight on his selected course. Then Nancy noticed that the ground was beginning to slope away from them. They were entering a small but deep valley.

The pilot coordinated stick and rudder and rolled into a gentle spiral. "There's a dry riverbed below," he said. "It's large enough for us to set down on."

Nancy fought to remain calm as Bruce continued his descending turn. The walls of the valley seemed to be only inches from the plane's wing tips.

"Brace yourself!" Bruce cried, as he rolled the craft out of the turn. "We're coming up on the final approach!"

Nancy could now see the riverbed before them. It appeared to be smooth and long enough for a normal landing. Suddenly, as the plane's wheels were about to touch earth, the alert girl spotted a fissure stretching across the width of the riverbed.

"Watch out!" Nancy shouted.

Bruce reacted immediately. He pulled back

hard on the stick. Luckily, the plane had enough speed to take to the air again and leapfrog the fissure. The craft settled back to earth. The pilot applied brake and brought it to a stop.

The fliers sat in silence for a minute or two. Nancy was the first to speak. "Congratulations," she said. "That's what I call doing the impossible."

Bruce blushed slightly. He climbed out of the plane and opened the cowling.

Nancy glanced at the fuel gauges. "Why do you think the engine quit?" she asked. "Our tanks are more than half full."

"The reason is pretty clear," Bruce replied as he examined the plane's engine. "I picked up a lot of dust and sand, chasing after John Wade's colt. It clogged the carburetor."

Nancy helped the pilot make repairs. Soon the engine was running smoothly again and the two fliers lost no time taking off out of the valley.

The search went on. Finally Bruce was heading across a hilltop with a rather steep descent at the bottom. The ground was covered with gravel, stones, and low-growing bushes.

"Oh!" Nancy exclaimed suddenly. "I think I see something!"

She grabbed the binoculars and trained them out the window. "There are John Wade and his pony!" she said. "I hope they're all right."

Bruce made a turn, came back, and looked from

his window. The man and the animal were lying still at the bottom of the slope. The noise of the plane did not arouse them. They remained motionless.

"Let's go down and see what the trouble is," Nancy urged.

Bruce descended but had to land some distance from the foot of the hill. He and Nancy climbed out quickly and ran back.

Bruce began calling out, "John! Are you all right?"

There was no reply.

Bruce and Nancy raced on, fearful that the prospector and his pony might not be alive!

CHAPTER XIV

A Frightening Message

AT ONCE Nancy dropped to her knees and felt John Wade's pulse. It was a little weak but steady.

"He's only unconscious," she reported.

In the meantime Bruce had thoroughly examined the pony. "She's got a nasty bump on the head, probably from a stone. But I think she'll come around. I'll run back to the plane and get my first-aid kit."

When the pilot returned, he took a restorative from the kit, broke it open, and held it under John Wade's nostrils. Almost at once the man shook his head, then opened his eyes. A bit dazed, he looked up at the couple.

"Thank goodness you're all right," Bruce said, and moved over to give the pony the same restorative treatment.

Fifteen seconds later the animal snorted, then started to get up. She did not rise on the first attempt. Apparently she was still weak. It took several tries, but finally she staggered up.

"You're going to be all right, little gal," Bruce said, patting the animal's neck.

"I'm glad of that," John Wade said.

He did not endeavor to stand up, preferring to regain his strength while still seated. He asked Nancy and Bruce to sit down with him so he could tell them what had happened.

"When my pony and I reached the top of the hill, the earth suddenly gave way. There was a small landslide, which carried us down to the bottom. We banged our heads and passed out. But how did you happen to be here?" he asked Nancy and Bruce.

They told John Wade about their forced landing, then Nancy added, "I have a surprise for you, Mr. Wade." She smiled. "I'm sure you're going to be delighted to hear it."

She related her adventure in the cave, the scurrying of the mice, and the shower of oil, which started and stopped abruptly. "The oil seeped into the ground rather quickly, but left enough on the floor to make it slippery. It's too bad I didn't bring a sample to show you."

During her story John Wade kept staring at her and listening intently. Finally he said, "Oil? I can't believe it. There must be a most unusual formation in that hillside."

He stood up, all his vigor restored. The prospector turned to his pony. "Let's go back and see that place ourselves! Why, there may be a fortune waiting for us!"

Suddenly he stopped and looked at Nancy. "But I don't deserve this oil. You discovered it."

Bruce spoke up. "That's right. Finders keepers."

Nancy surprised Mr. Wade by saying, "I'm the daughter of a lawyer and I've picked up a few ideas from him. The oil I found was not from underground but overground, so to speak. Somebody must own that hill, but I'm sure you could make an arrangement with the person to share the oil. Of course, I believe some of the profit has to go to the government."

John Wade shook his head. "You're quite a girl," he said. "But I still say you're the finder, not I."

Nancy immediately set the man's mind at rest by telling him she was not interested in sharing any profits from her discovery. "It was an exciting adventure, and that's all I care about."

Bruce asked the prospector if he really felt well enough to travel. "Your pony seems okay," he added.

John Wade laughed. "I feel fit as a fiddle."

Nancy and Bruce decided to leave. They said good-by and wished him luck with his oil venture. The couple walked to their plane and flew back to Excello.

As they went toward the area where Bruce's car was parked, they saw Hal Calkin coming toward them. He stopped and grinned at Nancy.

In his rapid speech he said, "Whatdidyoudoto-yourself? Fallinanoilbarrel?"

Nancy's eyes sparkled. Speaking as fast as he did she answered, "No. AlotofmiceandItookaslippery-trip." Bruce roared with laughter, but Hal merely stood there, looking puzzled.

When Nancy reached the Hamilton ranch house, she decided to go up to her room through the back door to avoid being questioned by other people. When she reached it, no one was there. Apparently Bess and George were not back from their horseback-riding trip with Chuck and Range.

During the past several hours, the cousins and their escorts had been having an unusual adventure of their own. For a while they had followed the well-trodden trails. Then the boys suggested going up a hillside and into a grove of aspen trees.

"There's a spring of delicious water in there," Chuck said.

"Wonderful!" Bess replied. "Why don't we eat our lunch by the spring?"

The others agreed. They took the saddles and other gear off their ponies and hung them on limbs. The animals were tethered on long leads.

George was amused at the antics of her mount. Finding himself free, the pony jumped up and down several times, then lay on the grass and rolled over and over.

Bess giggled. "Wouldn't you think he had had enough exercise climbing that hill?"

Her horse was standing perfectly still. He put down his head and seemed to be going to sleep.

"Chuck," Bess asked, "what do you call a horse's siesta?"

Chuck shrugged and grinned. "I guess only Spanish horses are allowed to have siestas. American ponies just take a rest."

The others laughed and Bess said, "I stand corrected."

The saddlebags containing the riders' lunch and Thermoses of milk were opened. The little group sat down, facing the direction from which they had come.

The panorama before them was intriguing. Hills and valleys were interspersed. Off in the distance the young people could see the great cloud.

"I wonder how Nancy made out," George said. "Let's hope she picked up some good clues."

Range said, "What's a good clue as opposed to a bad one?"

Bess and George looked at each other. They had never thought of this, but finally George said, "I suppose a bad clue would be a misleading one."

"I see," he said. "A good clue would lead you right to the bad guy."

Bess and George smiled and agreed that a good

clue eventually led to the villain, but sometimes the way was not very well marked.

"But Nancy Drew is the kind of detective who doesn't give up until a mystery is solved," George explained.

By this time lunch was spread out and the picknickers helped themselves to ham and cheese sandwiches, cole slaw, big pieces of angel food cake, and milk.

"Do you think Roger Paine will ever be found?" Range asked.

"I hope so," George answered, "but it seems very strange to me that he has never communicated with anyone, and yet we know he didn't have a plane accident."

Bess added, "Which means, as Nancy suspected, that he must have been kidnapped!"

Both cowboys said they thought it unusual that no demand for a ransom had been received if Roger had been abducted.

George replied, "There may have been some reason other than money for kidnapping him."

"Like what?" Chuck asked.

Before anyone could answer, there was the crackle of twigs behind them. The four young people turned around quickly. A man, his big hat pulled low, ambled toward them!

Bess, George, and the boys jumped up.

"Who are you?" Chuck called out.

The plodding figure came on without replying,

but just before reaching the group, he raised his hat.

"Ben Rall!" Bess cried out.

Under his breath Chuck asked Bess, "Is this the man who you think planned to kidnap Nancy the night of the masquerade?"

"Yes," she replied.

George wondered why the Hamilton ex-cowboy had dared to appear. He must know by now that he was liable to a prison sentence since Pop had discovered he was a thief.

She asked him, "Did you come to give yourself up?"

"What do you mean? I ain't done nothin' wrong."

"Maybe you don't think it's wrong," George told him, "but I certainly think stealing is a criminal offense."

Ben flared up, "What the heck do you mean? I didn't steal nothin'. Pop gave me the pony."

"I'm not talking about the pony," George said. "How about the money you took from the other cowboys?"

The man glared at her. "I didn't steal nothin', I tell you!" he exclaimed. "And don't you or nobody else accuse me of being a thief!"

He was so vehement in his denial that George began to wonder if Pop Hamilton were wrong. Since no one had seen the theft, it was possible some stranger had sneaked into the bunkhouse and taken the money at about the time Ben had left.

Range said, "We'll give you the benefit of the doubt. Now tell us what you want."

Rall did not reply. Instead he pulled a sealed letter from his pocket and handed it to George.

She read aloud, "From Roger Paine to whom it may concern."

The two couples were astounded. At once they demanded to be told where Roger Paine was.

"I don't know," Ben replied. "Honest I don't."

"How did you get this note from him?" George asked.

"I didn't," Ben answered. "A messenger brought it to me."

Bess wanted to know why he had brought the note to them. "Why wasn't it sent to his parents?"

Ben said he had been told to deliver it to Nancy Drew or someone in her group. "And that's all I know!" he shouted angrily. "Don't ask me any more questions."

Then, as an afterthought, he added, "If Roger's family, or his friends, or any of you people get any funny notions in your heads about hunting for him, there'll be trouble. I was told to give you that message, too."

"How did you know where we were?" Bess asked.

"I trailed you," he replied.

George now examined the envelope thoroughly. On it was printed, "The person who bears the answer to this note must come alone and unarmed. He will meet Ben at this spot."

Chuck and Range began to question Ben about this. Range said, "I suppose you're being well paid to do this job."

Ben shouted at him, "That's none of your business and you'd better not be so snoopy!"

Chuck said, "Ben, you could get into a heap of trouble over this. Aren't you afraid you might be arrested?"

For a brief second the ex-cowboy looked frightened. Finally he said, "No, I ain't. I got friends. They'll protect me."

George asked him, "Suppose you should be followed from here by unfriendly riders. What would you do?"

This time there was no question but that Ben was frightened. Turning on his heel, he ran off quickly through the wood. At the edge of it, he jumped onto his pony and raced away.

Chuck said, "Shall we chase him?"

Both Bess and George thought this would be the wrong thing to do, and Bess added, "We have the note. Right now that seems to be the important thing. Let Pop Hamilton attend to Ben."

A discussion followed as to who should open the note.

"Should we save it for Nancy?" Bess asked. "Or how about Pop Hamilton?"

George said this would be all right, but the boys felt that they should take the note to the police.

"That will take a long time," George said, "and I feel this demands action. It says on the envelope, 'To whom it may concern.' We're concerned. Why don't we open it?"

The others agreed and Bess slid one finger under the pasted flap. She pulled out a small sheet of paper.

"What does it say?" George asked.

Bess read aloud:

To get my freedom I must hand over my plane and $4,000.00. Bring the money to Ben Rall at the Buffalo Spring on Thursday morning. If the police are notified, I will be killed.

Roger Paine.

CHAPTER XV

Bess's Dilemma

"LET's call Mr. Paine—Roger's father!" Bess exclaimed. "This is perfectly dreadful!"

George and their companions, Chuck and Range, agreed. The four studied the ransom note for some time. George even held it up to the light to see if there was a clue to the writer on the paper. She saw nothing.

Range asked, "Is it genuine?"

Chuck shrugged. "It could be a forgery. I've never seen Roger Paine's handwriting, but the message sounds phony."

Bess suggested that Pop Hamilton might have seen the missing man's handwriting, so they decided to ride straight to the ranch. They kept talking about the strange note.

Chuck asked, "If Roger Paine didn't write it, do you suppose Ben Rall did?"

"You mean to get the money for himself?" Bess asked. "But why four thousand dollars?"

Chuck said he would not put it past the cowboy. "The men who work at Hamilton Ranch think he's dishonest. And this would be a way for him to make some easy money."

George was skeptical of this explanation. She asked, "What would Ben do with an airplane? He's not a pilot, or even a student."

"He might try to sell it," Range replied.

George said, "He'd have to turn over certain ownership papers and then he'd be caught, wouldn't he?"

"Sure he would," Chuck replied. "Ben Rall isn't too bright, though, and he might not know this."

The foursome rode along in silence for a while, then George said, "I'm eager to show this note to Nancy. She'll have some interesting thoughts about it, I'm sure."

The others could not argue against this, but had not given up the idea that Pop Hamilton should read the message as soon as possible.

"If he finds out it's genuine, he'll know how to proceed," Bess said.

As soon as they reached the ranch, Chuck and Range inquired where Pop was. They were told that he was far away, checking cattle. He was not expected back for some time.

Bess and George thanked the boys for the ride and Bess said, "Chuck, riding with you is always exciting. But this time had all others beat.

Imagine having a ransom note delivered to us!"

When the cousins reached their room, they found Nancy in the bathtub, with bubble-bath foam up to her chin. Her hair was soaking wet and she announced with a chuckle that she had just had an oil shampoo.

At this moment George spied a heap of messy clothes in one corner of the bathroom. "What's this?" she asked.

Nancy grinned. "They're the things I wore today. I'm not sure I'll ever get them clean."

"You had an adventure!" George exclaimed.

"Tell us about it!" Bess said.

Nancy explained exactly what had happened to her in the cave. When she reached the part about the mice coming out of everywhere and scurrying to the exit, George roared with laughter, but Bess squealed and made a face.

"Ugh!" she said. "I'm glad I wasn't there with you. But, Nancy, didn't they frighten you out of your wits?"

"They certainly startled me," Nancy admitted. Then she added, "Bess, you won't believe this, but those mice had more sense than I did. They seemed to know when it was going to rain oil in that cave and scooted. Of course I had no idea of such a thing and got caught in the shower."

George threw back her head and laughed even louder. "What a picture! Oh, Nancy, stop please, you're making me cry!"

The girl detective went on with her story of how she had been almost trapped by the slippery oil on the stone steps in the cave.

"That reminds me," she said. "My sweater, which probably saved my life, is still in the container in Bruce's plane."

Bess suggested she leave it there. "Most people who work around planes don't mind oil," she said. "Don't they call them grease monkeys?"

"And that's not all," Nancy said, laughing. "After the cave experience, Bruce and I had a forced landing in the plane."

"A what?" George asked.

Nancy went on to tell her friends about the riverbed episode.

"Hypers!" George exclaimed. "I'll say it again, you had your share of adventures today." She suggested that Nancy get out of the tub now, have a good rubdown, and put on some fresh clothes.

"We have something really important to show you," Bess said, "but we can't let it get all wet."

Nancy's interest was aroused at once. "What is it that's so important?"

George winked at Bess, and the two girls kept quiet.

"So you're not going to tell me until I'm dressed?" Nancy said. "Okay, give me five minutes and I'll join you."

Bess and George went back into the bedroom and combed their windblown hair. In a few minutes Nancy appeared, this time in a robe and slippers. She sat down in a tufted chair and curled her feet up under her.

"Now I'm ready for your big story," she said. "Which one of you is going to tell me, or are both of you?"

Bess and George looked at each other. Finally Bess said to her cousin, "You be the one."

"Okay." George told about the meeting with Ben Rall and his denial of the theft. "Then he handed me this." She pulled the ransom note from her pocket and gave it to Nancy.

The cousins waited while she read the ransom demand a couple of times.

Impatient for a comment, Bess asked, "What do you think of it? Is the note authentic?"

"I'm inclined to think so," the young detective replied. "I've been expecting something like this all along. But I must admit, having the note delivered to you by Ben Rall was unexpected. I wonder why." Then Nancy asked, "Where is the Buffalo Spring?"

George told her it was at the same spot where they had received the ransom note. "It may be a hiding place for Ben," she suggested. "But he galloped away so fast on his pony that we don't know where he went."

Nancy smiled. "Perhaps to Roger Paine's abductor. Probably Ben works for the kidnapper. It's too bad you didn't have a chance to follow Ben, or at least see which direction he took."

George put in, "Nancy, who do you think is

supposed to pay the four-thousand-dollar ransom? The only thing the note says is 'To whom it may concern.' "

Nancy admitted that from every angle the four-thousand-dollar demand puzzled her.

"It's a small sum for anyone to ask for a hostage and if the abductor has to share the money with Ben, and possibly others, this wouldn't leave much for himself."

George agreed, then said Chuck had suggested that Ben and some pal might be planning to keep the money.

Nancy replied they could not do much until Pop Hamilton or someone else who knew Roger Paine's writing could identify it. "Possibly the manager at Excello can."

Suddenly Nancy changed the subject. She said she had almost forgotten to tell the girls an important bit of news. "I figured out the last word in the message on the medal!"

"You did!" the cousins exclaimed together.

They waited for Nancy to go on. She said, "It's cloud.' "

In unison the three girls recited the whole sentence: "Revolution bomb site under great cloud."

George added, "Now at least we know where the bomb site is. But what does the message mean?"

"It means," Nancy replied, "that we'll have to do a lot more searching before we fully understand what we're after."

Optimistically Bess asked, "Nancy, when you've been out in that area with Bruce, have you ever seen anything that would give you a clue?"

"Not a thing," the girl detective replied. She said a new thought had just come to her, however. "As soon as Ned, Burt, and Dave arrive at the ranch, let's go out there, where the big cloud is, and make a thorough search."

At once George was enthusiastic about the idea. "I'm all for that!" she replied.

Bess, on the other hand, became very quiet. Nancy looked in her direction for some comment on the proposed trip. Tears were trickling down Bess's cheeks, and she was trying hard not to cry.

George asked her, "What's the matter? You're not afraid to go, are you?"

"No—oh no," Bess replied. "It's not that. It's just that——"

Bess could not go on. She burst into tears.

Nancy and George were puzzled. Bess lifted her tear-stained face. "It's just that——" Her voice became very emotional. "It's just that I don't want Chuck and Dave to meet!"

Nancy and George were stunned. Both of them had figured that the friendship between Bess and Chuck would come to a natural end when the girls were ready to leave the ranch. Apparently she was still thinking of marriage!

Finally Nancy went over to Bess and stroked her hair. "I had no idea you were so serious about

Chuck," she said. Bess did not reply, but she did stop sobbing.

Nancy glanced at her watch. "Soon it will be time for dinner," she said kindly. "I'll get dressed, then let's talk this over. In the meantime, honey, why don't you and George try to find Pop and show him the ransom note? I'm sure he's finished his work with the boys out on the range and is back by this time."

Bess got up, and though she said nothing, the worried girl went into the bathroom to splash cold water on her face. Then she daubed powder on her nose and brushed her hair again before she and George left the room.

Nancy stood lost in thought. The arrival of their Emerson College friends might turn out to be a problem. She hoped fervently there would be no confrontation between Chuck and Dave.

CHAPTER XVI

Buffalo Spring

WHEN Bess and George arrived at Pop Hamilton's office, they found that the rancher had just come in. He smiled genially at the cousins.

"Hello girls," he said. "Do you have a problem I can help you with? You look pretty excited."

"Something serious and scary has happened," Bess replied. "We came to tell you about it."

"Is it about the revolution bomb site?" Pop asked.

"No," George said. "But we did figure out the rest of the message."

"What is it?" Pop asked.

When the girls recited together, "Revolution bomb site under great cloud," the rancher frowned.

He looked down at the floor. "This is more serious than I thought," he admitted. "I must think about the best way to look into the situation."

He now changed the subject. "You said you had something to talk to me about?"

The cousins nodded and Bess said, "It concerns Ben Rall."

"You saw him?"

George spoke up, saying that the former Hamilton cowboy had come to the masquerade party uninvited and they were sure he had intended to kidnap Nancy.

Pop Hamilton scowled. "Why wasn't I told about this?" he demanded.

The girls informed him of the quick action of several guests at the party, who had hustled Ben outdoors and ordered him never to return.

"But today," said George, "while Bess and I were having a picnic lunch with Chuck and Range near Buffalo Spring, Ben Rall suddenly appeared out of the woods. He denied being a thief, then handed this note to me."

She took the envelope from a pocket and gave it to the rancher. "We wondered if you could identify the handwriting as Roger Paine's?"

Pop Hamilton stared at the envelope for several seconds, then he took out the note. As he read it, his mouth fell open, then his lips set in a grim line.

"I don't recognize this writing," he said. "Definitely, it is not Roger Paine's, and by the way, it is not Ben Rall's either. And this message is preposterous."

"More complications," George said.

At this moment Nancy walked into the office. Pop greeted her and repeated what he had just told Bess and George. "I wish I knew who did write this ransom note," he concluded. "Even a little hint would help."

Nancy asked Pop if he thought the writer could be the person who had kidnapped Roger Paine and perhaps taken his plane.

"That's a logical guess," Pop replied, "but I'm afraid that's all it is. Right now the only way I know how to get at this whole situation is to take Ben Rall into custody and get the truth out of him.

Nancy remarked that Ben had seemed very frightened of the person who had given him the note to deliver. She wondered if the cowboy would be too scared to divulge any secrets.

"He kept insisting he didn't know the person's name or anything about him or where Roger Paine is," she said.

Pop smiled. "Ben may be telling the truth, but I can still arrest him on the charge of being an accomplice in a kidnap case."

Nancy suggested that the deputy sheriff take someone with him to meet Ben. "He may have pals in hiding," she said.

After a few moments of thought, Pop said, "I'll take Chuck and Range with me. I can carry a package that will look as if it contains money.

Now don't you three worry your pretty heads over a thing. Just have a good time. I know you're excellent sleuths, but keep away from danger."

At this moment the dinner gong rang. The girls wished Pop good luck on Thursday, then went off to the dining room.

They lined up at the buffet and when they sat down at their table, Nancy's and George's plates were heaped with delicious food. Bess had only some soup, a roll, and a cup of tea.

Nancy asked kindly, "Don't you feel well, Bess?"

"I guess I'll be all right, but not for days and days," the girl replied. "To tell the truth, I'm too nervous to eat."

"About Dave?" George asked.

Her cousin confessed that she was apprehensive for two reasons. First, she was fearful that something would happen to Chuck while he, Pop, and Range were trying to capture Ben Rall. Second, her chest tightened and she felt a twinge of pain every time she thought of the moment when Chuck and Dave would meet.

George asked, "What do you think will happen? You don't believe that silly dream you had about the boys having a duel?"

"No, of course not," Bess replied. "They're both too intelligent for that. It's just that I don't want to hurt either one of them, and I don't know how to avoid it."

Nancy looked intently at her friend. "I have a feeling that way down underneath, Bess, you can't make up your mind whether or not you want to get married and give up your present way of life to stay out here."

Bess did not reply but Nancy felt certain she had hit upon the truth. She deliberately changed the subject and said, "Let's eat."

At first Bess drank her soup listlessly, but finally she finished it and started on the roll.

Nancy winked at George, then said, "I don't know why I took all this food. I never could eat it all. Bess, won't you please have some of my roast beef?"

"Oh, all right," she said.

George took the cue. As soon as Bess had finished the meat, her cousin said, "I'm as bad as Nancy. I haven't touched my salad, and it looks so good. Bess, please eat it for me."

Bess accepted the plate of fruit salad. With her appetite restored, she even went to the dessert table and picked out a large piece of blueberry pie.

Nothing more was said about food. Nancy suggested that the girls take horses the next morning and go for a ride. "I'm not scheduled for a flying lesson, so I can join you."

Bess and George said they would like that, so the following morning they went to the corral to get their ponies.

They learned from Pete that Pop, Chuck, and Range had left a couple of hours earlier. Pete added, "I'm sure hoping that by this time they've caught that mean rascal Ben Rall."

He helped the girls saddle their mounts. Once more Nancy chose Daisy D.

As the three riders set off, George asked, "Where are we going?"

Nancy replied, "I thought we might head for Buffalo Spring. We may be able to see the tail end of some excitement."

Bess could not make up her mind whether she wanted to go there or not. One moment she thought, "At least I could find out what happened to Chuck." The next second she was telling herself that if something dreadful had happened to him, she did not want to see it!

Nancy told her that since the men had had such a head start, the girls could never catch them. "What I'm hoping is that they'll bring back Ben Rall as a prisoner and we'll meet them."

Bess heaved a sigh. "I certainly hope you're right," she said, and followed as George led the way toward Buffalo Spring.

The girls made good time but did not meet anyone. There were no other riders to be seen and none of the planes from the Excello Flying School were in the area.

George remarked, "It's sure lonesome out here."

Nancy nodded and suggested that the girls have

a short race to give the horses a little extra exercise.

"See that clump of yucca ahead?" she asked. "Let's call that our goal."

The girls started out with Nancy in the middle lane. The ponies evidently enjoyed the sport, because in a few seconds they had put on top speed. Little by little Nancy and her mount edged ahead.

Then suddenly she saw something only a few feet before her. A deep gopher hole! If Daisy D should step into it, she would certainly break a leg!

Instinct told Nancy to turn her pony sharply to one side, but at this moment such a move would be disastrous. If she went to the left she would crash into Bess. If she turned to the right she would hit George!

Nancy had only one choice. She yanked on the reins so hard that Daisy D reared up almost straight, and for a moment the girl thought both she and the pony would twist over backwards!

But the animal's natural sense of balance made her come down with all four feet on the ground. She was less than six inches from the gopher hole!

"Oh, thank you, Daisy D!" Nancy murmured, and patted the horse's neck. "You're a great girl!"

In the meantime Bess and George had reached the clump of yuccas in a photo finish, then slowed down their mounts. They turned swiftly and cantered back to Nancy.

"What happened to you?" Bess asked.

Nancy told her.

"How awful!" Bess exclaimed. "I'm glad you weren't hurt."

George added, "Thank goodness nothing happened to either you or Daisy D."

Nancy smiled wanly and sat still to rest. The other girls were also quiet for a few seconds. Suddenly all three ponies cocked their heads.

"They must have heard something!" George remarked. "Listen!"

"I hear it too!" said Nancy.

The three riders concentrated on the sound. From somewhere in the distance came a man's pleading cry. "Help! Come here! Help me! Get me loose!"

CHAPTER XVII

Chilly Meeting

"THAT is a cry for help!" George exclaimed.

Nancy put a finger to her lips to indicate that the riders should be quiet and listen for another call. About ten seconds passed, then the faint plea came again.

"Help me! Help me!"

By this time the girls had figured out which direction the cries were coming from. Nancy and her friends started across the flat land, watching carefully for stones, gopher holes, and bushes with thorns. As they proceeded, the man's cries became louder, so they knew they were getting closer. The riders finally reached the foot of a wooded slope. The person who wanted help was apparently at the top.

"He must've had an accident," Bess remarked.

Nancy suggested that the girls leave their ponies behind and climb up. "In case this is a hoax of some kind," she said, "we should stick together and stay near the trees for hiding places."

"Good idea," George agreed.

When the girls reached the top, they paused, and Nancy called out, "Where are you?"

"Over here," was the reply.

She and her friends turned to the left and walked a few feet.

"Oh!" Bess cried out.

Before them, secured tightly to a tree with a lariat, stood Ben Rall! "Wal, thank goodness somebody showed up!" he said. "Come here and untie me!"

"Not yet," Nancy replied. "First, tell us who did this to you?"

Ben's answer was surprising. "It was Pop Hamilton!" the cowboy cried out angrily. "He's got no right! Let me loose!"

As Bess started to move toward him, Nancy grabbed her arm. "Not yet," she said. "Ben, tell us why Pop did this."

The man's eyes became like slits and he hissed, "Pop double-crossed me and left me here to starve!"

The girls doubted this. Nancy took a step forward and said, "Now suppose you tell us the truth!"

Ben Rall changed his attitude. Giving Nancy a sickening smile, he said, "I'll make a bargain with you. If you'll untie me, I'll give you the whole story straight."

Nancy did not believe him. She asked, "Where did you meet Pop?"

"At the Buffalo Spring," the cowboy replied. "But that's when he double-crossed me and wouldn't carry out the instructions in the note. He brought a package of money with him, but instead of handing it to me he got those fresh boys, Chuck and Range, to tie me up."

Nancy wondered if she should tell this man that she was sure Pop had told him that he was believed to be an accessory in a kidnapping. She decided not to, but was puzzled. If Ben's story was true, why didn't Pop return and take his prisoner into custody?

Just then Ben Rall began to laugh uproariously. The girls looked at him in surprise. What had brought about this change of attitude?

Finally, between chuckles and sighs, Ben Rall said, "Pop Hamilton thinks he's the smartest rancher in the whole West. Well, I'm here to tell you he ain't. He left me tied up while he and the boys went off to find the person who gave me that ransom note, but they don't stand a ghost of a chance of doing that. What's more'n likely to happen is they'll get themselves killed!"

Nancy was shocked by this announcement. Did Pop Hamilton know of the danger he was riding into?

Bess, in the meantime, had begun to tremble. She asked, almost in a whisper, "Did Chuck and Range really go off with him?"

"Sure they did. You may never see them again!"

Bess sagged against Nancy and then settled to the ground. George too was horrified by the man's statement. She said to Ben, "Just what do you mean?"

Ben roared with laughter again. "The two of 'em will likely get hung!"

This was too much for Bess, who screamed and then put her head in her hands. Burying her face between her knees she rocked back and forth in despair.

"I can't stand it!" she wailed.

Nancy was upset but she managed to ask Ben, "Where did you send Pop, Chuck, and Range?"

A sly look came to the man's face. "Let me go and I'll tell you!" he answered, his lips curling into a sneer.

Nancy informed the cowboy that Pop Hamilton was a deputy sheriff and tying Ben up was the same as putting him in jail. "If I let you loose, I'd be breaking the law. I can't do that."

Ben shrugged. "Have it your own way," he said. "But if you'll untie me, I'll lead you to the place where I sent Pop Hamilton and your boyfriends on their ponies."

Nancy did not answer, but Bess raised her head. "Nancy," she said, "isn't it worse to think of something happening to Pop, Chuck, and Range than it is of untying Ben?" She looked around. "He doesn't even have his pony, so he couldn't go far away if he escapes."

"That's right," the man said. "What's more, Pop took my gun. Now I ain't got nothin' to defend myself with. So you see, you have nothing to worry about. Untie me!"

Bess looked pleadingly at Nancy. "Please!" she begged.

Nancy did not know what to do. There might be some truth in what Bess was saying. On the other hand, Ben could easily get away from the three girls. She had a hunch his pony was hidden close by, even though the girls could not see it.

"Listen!" George cried out. "I hear hoofbeats."

Were the oncoming riders Pop and the boys, or friends of Ben's?

"Let's hide!" George urged.

For safety the three girls ran behind trees. In a few minutes their worries were over. Riding toward them were Pop, Chuck, and Range, all of them unharmed!

Nancy and the other girls came out of hiding. The riders were amazed to see them.

"Well. I'll be a gopher's uncle!" Chuck exclaimed.

"How did you get here?" Pop asked the girls.

"On the backs of three ponies," Nancy replied. She grinned. "We came to see if you had captured the man you were after. We found him tied up but wondered where you had gone."

Ben was mumbling to himself but the girls could catch only the words "cowgirl," now and then, and "Hate the whole bunch of 'em."

"Your prisoner begged us to let him go and even promised to lead us to you," Nancy said.

Pop Hamilton glared at Ben, then said to the girls, "I'm glad you didn't let this slippery eel go. He's not to be trusted."

Bess spoke. "I'm glad none of you got hurt as Ben said you would."

George asked, "Did you find the kidnappers?"

Pop shook his head. "We took a chance following a direction Ben told us to go, but of course he wasn't telling the truth."

The rancher suggested that the girls continue their ride. He and the boys would take the prisoner to town and have him locked up. "Then maybe he'll talk!"

"You can't do that!" Ben shouted. "All I did was deliver a message and didn't even get paid for all my trouble."

He was told that he was wanted as a material witness, if not an accessory to the kidnapping. Apparently Ben had forgotten this possibility. He said no more, but glared at his captors.

As the girls were about to walk off and descend the slope, Chuck called out, "See you at the barbecue tonight!"

Range said he would be there promptly. "George, don't be late!"

The girls rode back to the ranch house. During the afternoon they all wrote letters home, then bathed and dressed for the evening cookout. They looked very attractive in their cowgirl costumes.

George chuckled. "If Ben Rall could see us now, he'd sure say he hated cowgirls dressed up!"

Nancy sighed. "I have a feeling that Ben is only a small part of the whole mystery of Roger Paine's disappearance and the sky phantom. How I wish we could get a break in the case!"

The three friends went to the lobby. Chuck and Range were waiting for Bess and George. For a moment Nancy felt a bit lonesome. She wished Ned were there, or even Bruce.

As the five young people stepped outdoors, they saw a small plane coming in for a landing on a nearby field. It set down, taxied toward the ranch house, and then stopped. A moment later Ned, Burt, and Dave stepped out.

"Oh!" the girls cried out together, and all of them started to run toward their Emerson College friends.

"Hi!" they called out.

Nancy quickly outdistanced the others, because Chuck had grabbed Bess's arm, and Range had taken hold of George's, slowing their progress.

Ned swept Nancy into his arms and kissed her. "I'm so glad to see you!" he said. "And what a beautiful suntan!"

"It's wonderful to see you, too!" Nancy replied.

"You're just in time to help solve a big mystery we've come across."

Ned, who was a tall, attractive football player, grinned. "I can't wait to start." He doubled up as if he were rushing a ball. "Where's the enemy's goal line?"

By now Bess and George had broken away from their escorts and hurried forward. Dave looked admiringly at Bess and said, "How's my cowgirl doing?"

George and Burt's greeting was a little more formal, but too warm to suit Range. The new-comers were introduced to the ranch boys, but Chuck and Range were aloof. Ned received a hearty handshake, however.

As they all walked back toward the ranch house, Nancy took Ned aside and in whispers told him about Bess's plight.

"I could see right away that something was wrong," Ned replied. "I don't like this kind of situation. It could mean trouble."

The Emerson boys checked in. Then they went to their room to unpack and change into more appropriate clothes for the barbecue than those they had worn on the plane trip.

Many people were milling around and were very sociable. After Nancy's group had filled their plates, however, they went off a little dis-tance by themselves. It was evident that conversa-tion was strained. Nancy and Ned tried to make this less noticeable by talking about the boys' trip to the ranch, then by completely analyzing the mystery of the sky phantom, the strange cloud, and the kidnapping of Roger Paine.

When Nancy's report had been discussed from every angle, Ned changed the subject and asked about Nancy's flying lessons.

"I'm getting along very well, according to my instructor," she answered. "He thinks I'll be ready to solo in a little while."

"That's great," Ned replied. "I can't wait to see you manipulate the stick."

As soon as the barbecue was over, Chuck and Range stood up and said good-night to the others. They did not smile or say anything to show that the visitors were welcome guests at the Hamilton Ranch.

Bess had controlled herself very well during the evening, but as soon as the girls reached their room she flung herself on the bed and sobbed.

"Oh what am I going to do?" she said. "This is awful—just awful!"

George, who was less emotional than her cousin, said severely, "You're going to get a good sound rest. Don't open your eyes until morning. If you keep on crying like this, you're going to look like a hollow-eyed ghost!"

Nancy, more sympathetic, added, "Please try to relax and calm down. Let tomorrow take care of itself."

Despite their worries, the three girls did sleep well, but awoke early. While waiting for the Emerson boys to appear for breakfast they walked outdoors. Pop was just coming in.

"Mornin', girls," he said cheerfully. Then he winked at them. "I sent Chuck and Range off on a special assignment across the hills. It'll take them all day." Without waiting for any comment, he strode into the ranch house.

Nancy thought, "What a wise man he is!"

As the girls looked after him, they saw their friends from home coming outside. There were greetings all around, then Nancy asked if the boys had slept well.

Dave's reply was, "Chuck and Range did, but I didn't. Someone put nettles in my bed!"

CHAPTER XVIII

The Amazing Cache

DAVE said no more about the nettles in his bed, but Burt burst out, "He thinks Chuck did it!"

At once Bess came to the defense of her cowboy friend. "He wouldn't do such a thing!" she declared. "I just know he didn't do it."

Nancy spoke up too in Chuck's defense. She told Dave that the Hamilton Ranch cowboy was a very fine person. Though he was jealous of Dave's friendship with Bess, Chuck would not play a mean trick on him. "Certainly not one like putting nettles in a bed," she added.

"I'm not sure," Dave replied. He said he still felt pretty uncomfortable from the prickles. "I've had two baths, but my skin's itching and stinging. I must have a million punctures in my back."

"I'm so sorry," said Bess. "Maybe the discomfort will wear off soon."

The six young people went in to breakfast and

by the time the meal was over, Dave seemed to feel like himself again.

As they got up and walked toward the lobby, Nancy said, "I have a little errand to do. Will you all excuse me? I won't be gone long."

"Promise?" Ned teased.

"Promise," she responded.

The group expected her to tell them what her errand was but the young detective did not explain. Nancy walked to the bunkhouse. Most of the cowboys had left for their day's work but in one area of the building she could hear voices. Nancy stood at the doorway and listened.

A man was saying, "That was a rotten trick to play."

"He deserved it!" another cowboy replied.

The first man went on, "Pop expects all of us to be gentlemen, Stevie. That includes not playing annoying tricks on guests at this ranch."

"I don't care," Stevie replied. "I hate these dudes that come here from the coast. They think they're pretty smooth. They need to be taken down a peg."

Nancy wondered, "Are they talking about our Emerson friends?"

Stevie went on, "That guy Dave came out to steal Chuck's girl, and I aim to fix it otherwise. And don't ask me to apologize to him. Listen, if you squeal——"

Nancy did not wait to hear the rest. She ran all

the way back to the ranch house lobby, where her friends were talking. Breathless, she hurried up to them.

"Chuck didn't put those nettles in your bed, Dave," she said. "It was a cowboy named Stevie." Nancy related what she had just overheard at the bunkhouse.

"Where is he?" Dave asked, excited. "I'll go there right now and have it out with this Stevie!"

"Please don't," Bess begged him. "Let Pop Hamilton settle this."

Dave finally agreed, and Nancy went off to find the rancher and report to him. She met him coming outside. Pop said he was looking for Nancy and her friends.

"Did you want to see me?" he asked.

Nancy said yes, told him about the nettles, and identified the perpetrator. "I don't want to be a tattletale, but——"

Pop interrupted her. "I'm glad you told me. I'll see to it that no more pranks are played on your friends." He frowned. "I don't allow this kind of nonsense around here."

He walked with her to the others in the group and said with a smile, "If you all plan to go riding this morning, I have a chore for you. Any takers?"

"What is it?" Burt asked.

"Up in the west field there are two cows with newborn calves. I'd like the four of them brought down here."

"I'd love to see the calves," Bess said. "I'll bet they're darling."

Dave asked, "But what do you do with a new-born calf?"

Pop laughed. "Don't worry. The mother will take care of her baby. You'd be surprised at how strong a day-old calf is. It can travel for miles and miles. But sometimes a timber wolf will attack and kill it. The animal will be safer here."

Bess, George, Burt, and Dave agreed to do the errand. Nancy told Pop she would be taking a flying lesson and hoped that Ned would go along to watch her at the controls.

Ned accepted the invitation with a broad smile. She wondered why he was grinning. Did he think all this flying business was a joke and that she was not much of a pilot?

"I'll show him," she thought, and smiled back.

Pop offered to drive Nancy and Ned to the flying school, so in a few minutes the group separated. Burt and Dave went to choose ponies for their ride, while Nancy and Ned were driven to Excello in a ranch wagon.

Bruce was waiting for Nancy at the school's office. She introduced Ned and asked Bruce, "Could we possibly take up a four-seater today? I'd love to have Ned go along."

"I think so. Let me check."

He consulted the flight-schedule board, then

made a request of the manager. Bruce came out of the office a few minutes later and said, "Everything's okay. We'll take *Lady Luck.*"

Ned Nickerson said he hoped the craft would live up to its name. Then he maneuvered Bruce aside and whispered something to him. The pilot asked a couple of questions, then nodded. Both young men smiled and returned to Nancy. Neither told her what had been said and she did not ask.

In a few minutes the trio was ready for take-off. Nancy's performance with the plane was so smooth and effortless that Ned was delighted. "I see Bruce is a great instructor," he commented.

The flying-school pilot responded with a twinkle in his eyes. "And Nancy is a great student."

The girl flyer blushed a bit and headed the craft toward the great cloud. As they neared it, Nancy told Ned about the mystery and the Indian legend. She ended by saying, "We think it's a hideaway for the sky phantom when anyone else is nearby."

Ned remarked, "That's a fantastic story. I wonder how the sky phantom gets through when all the electrical equipment in your plane went haywire."

"That's part of the mystery," Nancy replied. "I hope that pilot doesn't show up for a while, so we can investigate on the ground."

She set down at the nearest suitable spot, which was about quarter of a mile from the edge of the giant cloud.

Bruce said, "With all the strange things that have been happening lately, I think it best if I stay here and guard the plane. You go off and investigate."

Nancy and Ned headed directly for the area beneath the cloud. When they reached the area below the edge of it, the couple began searching the ground minutely. Almost directly under the middle of the cloud, Nancy stopped abruptly. Excited, she called Ned to her side and pointed at the area.

"Here's a spot that looks newly dug," she said, "and newly raked over. Do you think something might have been buried here?"

Ned nodded. "Let's see if we can find anything underneath?"

At once the two began digging up the dirt with their heels and fingers. In a few minutes they made a discovery. They had unearthed a long, narrow wooden box. Painted on the top of it was the word "RIFLES."

Nancy and Ned were so astonished they just stood still, staring first at each other, then down at the marked box.

"Let's see if there's anything else hidden here," Nancy urged.

They hunted around and came to a section that

had not been tampered with recently, but looked different from the surrounding area. The grass growing over it was very short and sparse compared to the longer growth around it.

"Want to dig here?" Ned asked.

"Yes."

Again the two sleuths dug their heels into the dirt. It was sun-parched and dry, and harder to dislodge than the other spot. Ned kicked at it vigorously with his heel while Nancy brushed aside the loose dirt and felt around in the hole he had made. Presently her efforts were rewarded.

"Ned, I think I've found a second box!" she said, excited.

Together they worked vigorously and a few minutes later had uncovered part of another box. Apparently this one was square. The two discoverers stared at the print on its lid.

BOMBS!

The couple's first thought was to run, in case they might have disturbed the cache and somehow triggered one or more of the bombs. But then Ned noted some more printing below the word "bombs." It was "DEFUSED."

"Wow!" he called out. "For a moment I thought it might be our last second on earth!"

"Don't think I wasn't scared too!" Nancy confessed.

At this moment they both heard a plane. Had

Bruce taken off? They looked in his direction but the craft was still on the ground.

"Somebody else is coming," Nancy exclaimed. "Maybe it's the sky phantom! If so, we mustn't let him see us!"

"There's no place for us to hide around here," Ned pointed out.

Nancy felt that the first thing they should do would be to heap dirt over the boxes. She and Ned worked frantically to do this.

The sounds of the oncoming plane were louder now. Suddenly an idea came to Nancy. Both she and Ned were wearing long-sleeved, dark sweaters and dark jeans. She suggested that they take their arms out, put them down inside their sweaters, and pull part of the knitted material over their heads.

"Then we'll curl up on the ground and hope we won't be spotted."

Quickly they did this, then waited, holding their breaths. Would the plane settle down near them? Was the pilot the sky phantom? Nancy listened carefully and was sure the sound was the same as that of Roger Paine's stolen plane.

Evidently its pilot had spotted the *Lady Luck*. It was doubtful that he had seen the two detectives on the ground, however, because while the craft dragged the area, it made no attempt to land. Instead, the plane went on and was soon out of sight. Nancy and Ned pulled their sweaters down.

"If that's the sky phantom, he mustn't see us!"
Nancy exclaimed.

He remarked, "Wow! That was a close call!" He laughed. "It's my first experience of suffocation because of an airplane flying overhead!"

Nancy chuckled. "There's a first time for everything! Well, I think we'd better get back to our own plane and report this whole discovery to Pop Hamilton. By the way, Ned, he's a deputy sheriff."

Bruce was standing outside the craft. He said, "I thought that plane was Roger Paine's, and I was afraid the pilot would spot you two. Thank goodness you're all right."

Nancy told him about their disguise and he laughed. "Very ingenious." After hearing the entire story, he said, "I suppose you want to get right back and report all this to Pop Hamilton."

"Yes, we do," Nancy replied.

To the girls' complete surprise Bruce now said, "Ned, how about your taking the controls?"

"I'd like to," the Emerson student replied with a wink at the girl detective.

Nancy stared unbelievingly at the two of them. "Are you kidding?" she asked.

Ned now admitted that he too had been taking flying lessons. "I couldn't let you get ahead of me!" he said to Nancy.

Ned proved to be an excellent pilot. When he brought the plane down smoothly on the flying school's runway, both Bruce and Nancy praised him.

She added, "That really was a marvelous surprise, Ned, and you kept your secret well."

Bruce drove them to the Hamilton ranch. Fortunately Pop Hamilton was near the entrance and heard their story. The rancher's eyes opened wide in amazement.

"Something must be done at once!" he exclaimed. "We must remove those buried rifles and bombs and try to capture the sky phantom and his buddies!"

Bruce, who had stood by, now spoke up. "I'm sure all my instructor friends at the school would be glad to help."

They discussed the best way to accomplish what they wanted to do. Several schemes were mentioned and discarded. It seemed to the flying group that the best way to catch the sky phantom was in the air.

Nancy said, "How about several planes surrounding the phantom flier when he comes? If he disappears into the cloud we can force him to surrender."

Bruce and Ned thought this was an excellent idea, and finally Pop was convinced.

Getting into the spirit of the game he said, "We'll start off at sunset."

CHAPTER XIX

Surprise Attack

BRUCE made some phone calls to the flying school to arrange for the sunset flight. He talked confidentially with the manager and asked if he would be willing to let certain planes and the instructors go on the mission the next morning.

After a long conversation, he came back to Nancy, Ned, and Pop, smiling. "Everything is arranged," he reported. "How about all you visitors going on the adventure?"

"That would be great," Ned replied. "Here come our friends now."

Bess, George, Burt, and Dave were just riding in. Walking behind them were two Brahman cows with their day-old calves. Pop and the others hurried forward to meet them.

As Bess slid from her pony, she said, "Aren't they adorable?"

"They certainly are," Nancy agreed.

She went up to one of the cows, patted her neck, then ran one hand up and down the calf's nose. He eyed her shyly, ready to bolt if she should try to stroke any more of his body. Two cowhands appeared and took charge of the animals.

"We'll put them in separate stalls for a little while," Pop said.

George now asked what Nancy and Ned had discovered. When the group heard about the couple's find, they were astounded.

"You actually uncovered rifles and bombs?" George asked incredulously.

Ned chuckled. He turned around and said, "Look at these heels of mine! They were my spade and rake." There was no doubt that the deep scuff marks on Ned's shoes had been made by hard digging.

Pop excused himself, asking Nancy to extend the invitation for the evening flight.

"We're going somewhere tonight?" Bess asked.

Bruce repeated Pop's offer. At once George, Burt, and Dave accepted.

Dave said, "I can hardly wait to help capture the villain and solve the mystery.

"Who do you suppose he's going to turn out to be?" Burt questioned. "The sky phantom, or some political terrorist?"

Nancy confessed that all she had done so far

was to eliminate suspects. "But within a few hours I hope we can catch the leader of the revolution," she added.

"And is he the sky phantom, or is the sky phantom his pilot?" Burt asked.

"I'm sure we'll soon find out," Nancy replied.

All this time Bess had said nothing. Finally George prodded her cousin into giving an answer about going on the sleuthing trip.

"If you want the truth," Bess said, "I'm scared to death. It sounds like war!" Then looking at Dave, she asked, "Do you want me to go?"

"I sure do," he replied.

It took several seconds for Bess to make up her mind, but finally she agreed to accompany the others.

Nancy and Ned lingered behind the rest as they set out for the ranch house. The girl detective had whispered to Ned that she wanted to inquire about Chuck and Range. Both at the corral and the bunkhouse she was told that the two cowboys had not returned.

She and Ned did not comment until they were out of earshot of everyone else. Then Nancy said, "Do you suppose Chuck and Range are staying away on purpose to avoid all of us?"

Ned agreed this was possible, but said with a smile, "You mean Dave and Burt. But personally I'd rather Chuck and Range didn't give in so easily. Running away from a problem isn't going to solve it."

No more was said on the subject. When the couple reached the ranch house, they separated to go to their rooms. Bess and George were already there. The blond girl was walking the floor and continuously running her hands through her hair.

George was a bit annoyed. "Oh Bess, for Pete's sake, stop walking around and trying to pull out all your hair! You may need it!"

Bess eyed her unsympathetic cousin but did not answer her. Instead she turned to Nancy and asked, "If you were in the predicament I am in, what would you do about it?"

At once her young detective friend replied, "I'd have a good talk as soon as possible with the boy who's the loser."

Bess answered at once, "But how can I talk to Chuck if he isn't here?"

Nancy smiled and George winked at her. "So you've decided on Dave?" Nancy asked. "That means you're not going to stay out here and marry Chuck?"

Bess said this was right. She had thought the matter over and while she was very attracted to Chuck she had concluded that in the long run Dave would be a better companion for her.

Nancy and George felt relieved, and Nancy

hugged Bess. "I'm glad," she said, and went to take a shower.

But George asked teasingly, "Bess, when did Dave ask you to marry him?"

Bess blushed to the roots of her hair. "He has never asked me, and maybe he never will, but right now he is my favorite boy friend."

George said, "Thank goodness."

Nancy was the first one to reach the lobby at suppertime. Ned was already there, and they walked outside to the garden. At once she told him about Bess's decision.

"I'd have felt pretty bad if she had decided against Dave," he remarked.

Nancy suggested, "I think it's best if Dave never finds out—or Burt either—how close Bess came to switching boy friends."

Ned nodded, then looking straight into Nancy's eyes, he added, "I'm glad you didn't toss me over in favor of Bruce!"

Nancy burst out laughing. "Little chance of that," she said. "Bruce has a lovely wife and an adorable baby!"

Ned chuckled too, then they walked back and went to the dining room. Conversation during the entire meal was about the upcoming trip.

At sunset the group gathered at the Excello field. Bruce, Nancy, Ned, and Pop were to occupy the plane that would lead the foray. The other couples were assigned to various craft.

After the rancher had taken his seat, he said to the others, "I have some news for all of you. After a great deal of trouble I got Ben Rall to talk."

Pop said that Ben had indeed stolen the other cowboys' money. He learned that the horse thieves were working for the man who had given him the ransom note. These men were supposed to cause all kinds of nuisances for Nancy's group and were responsible for various mishaps, as Nancy had suspected.

"Ben was a willing tool, but was never told much," Pop added.

Nancy asked, "Did Ben confess that he tried to kidnap me so I could be taken away?"

"Yes."

"Does Ben know who the sky phantom is?" Nancy inquired.

"Not exactly," Pop responded. "Ben declared that he does not know the name of the man who gave him the ransom note and to whom he was to deliver the money. He has never met the head of the gang. But he did find part of a torn message on the ground near the man's plane. It said the hidden stuff would be picked up at dawn on the twenty-eighth."

"That's tomorrow morning!" Nancy exclaimed.

"Exactly," the rancher agreed. "That's why it's a good thing we're going out now. We'll be ready for the sky phantom and his buddies."

Ned looked a bit grim. "These revolutionists will probably be armed," he said.

Pop admitted that they might be. "If there's any shooting," he said, "we'll turn back."

He now revealed that several deputy sheriffs were to be stationed around the area in case there was any trouble.

The six planes took off and followed Bruce, who was at the controls of the first plane. He led them to the scrubby land beneath the great cloud. The pilots had been instructed to form a circle when landing.

"I'm sure," he said, "that if the sky phantom sees our craft on the ground, he'll disappear into the great cloud. The rest of us will take off and surround him. Sooner or later he will have to come out and we'll force him to land."

There was bright moonlight, and Nancy and Ned decided to reconnoiter the vicinity. They carried bright searchlights with them and promised to return soon.

"First I'll show you the cave where we found Major," Nancy said and led the way.

They turned on their flashlights and went inside. Suddenly, somewhere ahead of them, they heard a low groan.

"Who's there?" Ned called out.

Before an answer came, he and Nancy were grabbed from behind. Two men whose faces they could not see knocked the flashlights from their hands. They punched the couple so that they fell forward. Then the attackers pulled large sacks over their captives' bodies.

Nancy and Ned struggled to get out, but it was hopeless. Both realized that the oxygen inside the bag would not last long. They would suffocate!

CHAPTER XX

The Sky Phantom

TIGHTLY wrapped in the stifling sacks, Nancy and Ned tried frantically to free themselves. Since they were not stopped, both wondered if their attackers had left. They could neither see nor hear anything.

"I must get out of here!" Nancy thought, becoming panicky.

It occurred to her that if she could not break out by using her fists and feet, she would have to pry herself loose from the cloth. Using her fingernails and her teeth, she began making holes in the covering.

Soon she had created an opening through which to breathe. At the same time Nancy began to worry about Ned.

Fortunately he had been tearing his way out of the sack just as she had. Soon each had torn a hole large enough to put his head through.

"Nancy! Are you all right?" Ned called out.

"Yes. And I'm so glad you are."

Both continued to shred the cloth until the opening was wide and they could crawl out. They felt around the floor of the cave for the flashlights. To their relief, the mysterious attackers had not taken them.

For a few minutes Nancy and Ned had completely forgotten about the person who was groaning in the cave. Had the men who tied them up taken him away?

The couple listened. Presently they heard the groans again. Nancy beamed her searchlight ahead while Ned trained his behind him in order to prevent another surprise attack.

Soon Nancy's light picked up the prone figure of a man trussed and gagged. He was lying on the floor at the rear of the cave. She and Ned hurried forward and quickly took off the gag.

Nancy recognized the person at once. "Roger Paine!" she exclaimed.

"Yes," he said in a shaky voice. "I was captured and hidden. Today I was brought here by a man who has the same initials as mine. I don't know his name."

Nancy now introduced Ned and together they untied the ropes that bound the prisoner.

"Thank you! Thank you!" Roger Paine said. He tried to get up but was too weak.

"We must take you out of here before the men who attacked us return," Nancy told Roger.

"If you can't walk, we'll carry you."

Roger said he knew he had lost a lot of weight. "The other R.P. brought me food and water once in a while," he said, "but not so much as I'm accustomed to eating."

It was decided that Nancy and Ned would carry the man, at least outside the cave. The fresh air seemed to revive Roger somewhat. Leaning on their shoulders, he was able to make it to the flying-school plane.

Bruce was amazed to see him. He was solicitous of his condition.

"Where's Pop?" Nancy asked.

"He went off to see about one of the other search groups. He hasn't come back."

Nancy suddenly looked at Bruce's right arm. "Why, what happened to you?" she asked in concern.

Bruce said he was afraid his arm was broken. "I was ambushed," he said. "Oh, I hope Pop and the others haven't been harmed!"

Ned climbed into the plane and immediately got in touch by radio with the other fliers. None of them had had any trouble. Right now Pop was with Bess, Dave, and their pilot.

"Tell him to come back here as soon as possible," Ned requested.

While waiting for Pop, Nancy and Ned gave Roger Paine some water and a box of crackers to eat. Then they brought out the first-aid kit and put Bruce's aching arm into a sling. They would take him to a doctor as soon as they reached the flying school.

"It feels much better now," the pilot said, wincing a bit.

As soon as Pop Hamilton arrived, Nancy said she wanted to make sure that the buried rifles and bombs were still at the site. Once more they hurried off with their flashlights, but this time took a small trowel and spade with them. It did not take long to find the exact spot and shovel away part of the dirt. They were relieved to find that the revolutionaries' hardware was still there, intact!

"This is some find," Ned remarked. "I can just see screaming headlines all over the nation."

The earth was smoothed over and the couple returned to the plane.

Bruce said, "Of course, with my broken arm I won't be able to pilot the plane. Nancy and Ned, you will have to do it."

Nancy's heart began to thump wildly as she thought of the task ahead of her but she looked at Ned, whose face was calm and unworried. Her courage was restored.

The four slept in *Lady Luck,* but awoke before dawn. They ate a quick snack and prepared for the day's adventure. The other five pilots reported that they were ready for action.

About five o'clock, Nancy heard another plane coming in their direction. "It must be the sky phantom!" she said. After listening to the rhythm of the craft, the girl detective was convinced she was right.

She and Ned took their places at the controls. Nancy sat in the pilot's seat. The engines of all the planes were revved up. As soon as the strange craft came into view, Ned tried to contact it. There was no answer.

"I guess it's time to go," he announced.

Nancy took the plane down the grassy runway and gradually rose into the air. All around her the other pilots were doing the same thing. Little by little they circled the strange plane until it was completely surrounded.

Once more Ned tried to contact the stranger, but again he received no response. Instead, the pilot of Roger Paine's craft found an opening between two planes and shot into the great cloud.

Pop Hamilton was impressed by the skill of Nancy and Ned as fliers. "We've got that villain boxed in!" he cried, excited.

The six planes flew round and round the edge of the great cloud and above and below it. Each craft had enough fuel to remain in the air for several hours. They hoped that their enemy would run out of fuel before they did.

Ned tried several frequencies, hoping to get a response from the enemy plane. Although there was none, he kept on pleading with the pilot to surrender and land.

"You haven't a chance," he said. Then to his companions he added, "This is maddening! We know Roger Paine's plane is equipped with a radio. I'm sure your sky phantom hears us."

There was no way of telling whether or not the mystery pilot had received their messages. All they could do was keep on flying. Sooner or later the stranger would have to come out of the great cloud and make a landing.

Pop spoke up, "If that guy suddenly emerges, and tries to get away we must chase him and force him down. I wonder where he'll come out."

Nancy guessed it would be underneath the great cloud. Then she thought the sky phantom would try to fly just above the ground until he was out of danger.

"He'll never be free of us!" Ned declared.

Nancy's hunch had been right. The enemy plane suddenly emerged from the base of the cloud and flew low over the ground to avoid the other craft. All the pilots were alerted. They too descended and gave chase. Gradually they managed to circle the enemy again.

When he realized it was impossible to get away, he let down his wheels and prepared to land. The other pilots picked spots and descended one by one.

Nancy and Ned had maneuvered their craft so they were closest to the man they were after. As soon as they taxied to a stop, Pop Hamilton opened the door and dropped to the ground. He raced toward the opponent's plane. Nancy and Ned were at his heels.

"Open up and get out!" Pop Hamilton ordered the sky phantom. "I am a deputy sheriff. You're under arrest."

Finally the door swung wide. A lean, dark-haired man with deep-set eyes and a swarthy complexion emerged.

"What's this all about?" he asked sullenly.

"Tell us your name," the rancher demanded.

"I'm not going to give you anything, and you have no reason to detain me," the man answered defiantly.

Pop Hamilton turned to Nancy. "Tell this man what you know about him."

The young detective said to him, "First of all, your initials are R.P. You stole Roger Paine's plane. Since you have the same initials, you thought you could get away with the theft."

The man's eyes blazed but he said nothing.

"Nancy, go on," Pop urged.

The girl's next remarks amazed the stranger. "You imprisoned Roger Paine but we found him. He's a short distance from here, and I'm sure he'll identify you."

The abductor's shoulders suddenly sagged, but still he said nothing. Nancy went on, "You are a member of a revolutionary gang. Under this big cloud you buried a lot of rifles and bombs."

Her remarks really shook the stranger. Panic

overcame him and he gazed around for a way to escape. He knew it was hopeless.

Finally he said, "How did you find out all this?"

Nancy explained about the medal he had dropped and how she and her friends had deciphered it. Now a look of real terror came over the man's face.

"You're too smart!" he shouted. "You can arrest me if you want to, but I won't tell you my name nor the names of anybody else I work with. I sent one of those medals to each of my friends, who knew the trick of reading the letters."

Ned offered to climb into the plane and see what he could find out. He was not gone long. In the pilot's compartment he discovered a booklet containing all the information Pop Hamilton would need to round up the revolutionaries. It also revealed that this man's name was Rudolph Panzer. Below it were the names and addresses of all members of the gang. Also included was a list of the contents of various boxes of firearms and bombs buried under the great cloud.

"There's enough stuff here to blow up the whole country!" Pop exclaimed.

Nancy stared at their captive for a moment, then said, "You may as well tell us everything. For instance, how did you make the mystery cloud magnetic?"

The stranger grinned. He almost seemed pleased by the young detective's question.

"That was easy," he said, boasting. "A scientist

friend of mine developed a super-fine magnetic dust. I merely *seeded* the cloud with it from my plane."

"Very clever," Nancy remarked.

"Clever enough to nearly put an end to you and that friend of yours!" Panzer declared angrily.

Ned fought hard to control his temper. "Never mind about that!" he put in. "Nancy checked with the state university climatology team that came out here twice and investigated the cloud."

"They concluded that it was formed from ordinary water vapor," Nancy interrupted. "How did you manage to throw the scientists off the track?"

"My plane is equipped with a special generator that produces a magnetic field of reversed polarity," Panzer said. "If anybody got too nosey about the mystery cloud, I would fly through it and turn on the generator. Presto! In a couple of minutes the magnetic dust was dissipated. I had you all fooled!"

"Not quite everybody," Pop added, winking at Nancy.

The girl detective asked Panzer about Ben Rall's part in the scheme.

"Nothing but a messenger, and he was a failure at that except bringing Major to us. Later he stumbled into our camp and we used him. The ransom demand was an idea of one of my men, and he sent it off without my knowledge."

Rudolph revealed that when Nancy and Bruce

had discovered Roger's plane, he had come with food to the imprisoned man, but moved him to another place after that. The skyjacker brought rifles and bombs to the site at daybreak, when no one was around. He was surprised to learn he had accidentally switched on the ELT system in Roger's plane when he landed.

Panzer glared at the girl detective. "If it wasn't for you," he snarled, "I would've gotten away with my scheme. You never found out about my dropping a pal of mine in a parachute. He always wears cowboy boots. Today, though, I came alone."

"You've said enough," Pop declared. "Put your hands behind your back." He slipped a pair of handcuffs over their prisoner's wrists. To the others he said, "Panzer and I will ride in one of the planes that had no passengers.

"Nancy and Ned, you go back to the ranch together. You will be commended for your work, but I want to be the first one to congratulate you on solving the mystery of the sky phantom."

Ned chuckled. "You mean Nancy solved it," he said generously. "I was just copilot and codetective."

"Thank you, Pop," said Nancy. "I admit there were scary moments."

Her days of frightening moments and adventures were not over. Very soon she would be launched on *The Strange Message in the Parchment.*

Right now she said to Pop, "I'll be glad when you catch the men who tied Ned and me up in those sacks, rolled the tree down the hillside to injure my friends and me, and killed Speed Boy."

"They're all members of the same gang, according to Ben Rall. We'll soon round them up. By the way, one of Panzer's pals had Ben Rall steal Major and sell it to him. The horse carried the heavy boxes from the plane to the holes Panzer dug. Later Ben used to spy on him. Then one day Panzer saw him and gave him the ransom note to deliver."

"I suspected that that was what happened," said Nancy. "The sooner you have the whole gang in custody the better. Pop, please congratulate Bess and George for me. Without them I never could have put all the pieces of the puzzle together."